all laced up

ERIN FLETCHER

Entangled Publishing, LLC
2614 South Timberline Road
Suite 109
Fort Collins, CO 80525
Visit our website at www.entangledpublishing.com.

Crush is an imprint of Entangled Publishing, LLC.

Edited by Heather Howland
Cover design by Syd Gill
Cover art from Shutterstock

Manufactured in the United States of America

First Edition October 2016

For Mom and Dad, who put skates on my feet and pencils in my hand.

Chapter One

LIA

I had taught young skaters before, but somehow I didn't think "Zamboni avoidance" was covered in basic skills class.

I skated toward the hulking machine that should have been re-surfacing the rough ice. Instead, it sat in the middle of the rink with its ancient hood hanging open, innards revealed.

"Mr. Kozlov?" I called, my voice echoing through the cold air of the empty rink.

"The Lia Bailey?" a voice called back from somewhere near the engine.

The Lia Bailey. He always preceded my name with the specifying article. Like I was someone. "It's me. What's going on?"

Mr. Kozlov's head and shoulders popped up behind the exposed engine. As usual, his white hair stood in seventeen different directions. Something black—grease, maybe?—covered his left temple, next to his bushy white eyebrows and kind blue eyes. "Old Bessie. She's sick."

Each Zamboni at The Ice House was named after a large animal, real or otherwise: Bessie, Shamu, Dumbo. I could never keep them straight, but Mr. Kozlov always did. "How bad is it?" I asked.

He disappeared back under the hood with some clanking sounds. "Don't know. Try to start her."

I carefully pulled myself up onto the machine using elbows and knees so I didn't have to step on anything with my exposed skate blades. I put one hand on the key in the ignition. "Now?"

"Now."

I turned the key, but all I received in response were some slow, mechanical grunts. Nothing about the grunts sounded encouraging.

Mr. Kozlov's head appeared again, the frown on his face accentuating his wrinkles.

"Maybe you should call someone to come look at it," I said.

He waved off the idea as if it were preposterous. "Takes too much money."

"But you'll have money after this workshop, right? That's the whole point?"

"Yes! And then I fix the heat in the boys' locker room! Or the roof in rink two, you know, where we put buckets every time it rains? Or maybe the scoreboard in rink three!" He laughs. "They complain the visiting team's score is eight. Always eight. I tell them eight is a good score in hockey, no?"

I was starting to think this ten-week workshop he'd asked me to teach needed to be more like ten years to pay for everything that needed to be fixed. When he'd mentioned the idea for the workshop, I'd volunteered right away. I'd do whatever it took to save the rink that was as much my home as my house. "What are we going to do about the kids? Is either one of the other rinks free at ten?"

"Hockey in both," came the muffled reply along with more clanking.

That was a good sign. The ice arena needed to stay busy on Saturday mornings during hockey season to keep the place afloat. But it didn't help my current predicament. I was about to have a bunch of tiny new skaters on the ice who presumably wouldn't be able to steer around Bessie or stop before crashing into her. If Mr. Kozlov couldn't afford a scoreboard, he definitely couldn't afford a lawsuit.

"Don't you worry," Mr. Kozlov said, "Bessie will be fixed before kids arrive."

Thankfully, he sounded more confident than I felt. "How many kids are you expecting?"

"Twenty-two!"

There was no way I heard that right. The last time we talked about the workshop, there were five kids registered with the possibility of a sixth. "I'm sorry, how many?"

"Twenty-two little skate cadets," he confirmed, like it was no big deal. "Try the engine again, please."

I didn't move, frozen in place by the impossibility of single-handedly pointing forty-four skates in the right direction and wiping twenty-two runny noses. "I thought you said there were going to be six!"

He just laughed. "The Lia Bailey! Turn the key, please."

Reluctantly, I did as I was told. From the sound of it, Bessie was just as reluctant as I was.

Mr. Kozlov popped his head back out for a second. "Don't you worry. Not twenty-two by yourself. You have a co-teacher."

It never failed to amaze me that Mr. Kozlov could memorize rink schedules and the past hundred years of hockey history, but couldn't remember to tell me things like the fact that I had a co-teacher for the workshop I thought I was teaching on my own. "Who's teaching with me?"

"Ah-ha!" Mr. Kozlov sounded thrilled about whatever he'd just discovered under Bessie's hood. "Problem fixed. Try her again."

"Who am I teaching with? Mackenzie?" Mackenzie and I weren't close friends—we didn't have many classes together and only occasionally saw each other at the rink—but it might be fun teaching with her. If nothing else, she could handle eleven of the kids.

Mr. Kozlov slammed Bessie's hood shut with a confidence that suggested whatever he'd done had solved the problem. "Mackenzie's skates aren't dull enough," he said, as if that were an explanation. "Not Mackenzie. Start Bessie's engine!" When I didn't do as he asked, he shooed me off the seat, back onto the ice where I came from. "Your co-teacher is Pierce," he said. Then he started Bessie's engine, letting out an enthusiastic whoop as she purred to life.

I blanched. Pierce. There was only one Pierce I knew. It couldn't be him. Under no circumstances could I spend the next ten weeks teaching with the Pierce I knew. "Wait, Pierce? Pierce Miller?" I asked, but Bessie's engine was too loud, and Mr. Kozlov was already halfway down the rink, occasionally checking the ice behind him to make sure it was smooth.

I struggled to remember the last time I'd been forced to interact with Pierce Miller. Since he advanced from Troy Preparatory Academy's hockey team to USA Hockey's National Team Development Program, I'd seen a lot less of him. Less at the rink because his new team practiced at an ice arena in Plymouth, a few cities over, and less at school because of his travel schedule with the team.

And when I did see him? Pierce was very good at not giving me the time of day.

The last interaction I had with him was at the rink shortly after he'd secured his place on the NTDP team. A gaggle of hockey players and their parents had stuck around after

Pierce's practice to get his autograph. Everyone in the city of Troy knew Pierce was going to be The Next Big Thing in hockey and teenage athlete celebrities. But when I walked into the rink for my practice while his crowd of adoring fans was walking out, Pierce must have thought I had been left behind.

"Oh, I missed one?" he asked, Sharpie still in hand. He grabbed my water bottle, signed a signature too perfect to be anything other than practiced, and handed it back. When he smiled at me, he somehow managed to do it without even looking at me. "Gotta run," he said, "but thanks for the support!"

No acknowledgment that we'd shared the same ice rink for most of our lives. No recognition that we'd had two classes together freshman year. No noticing that I might be headed to practice of my own and just wanted something to drink.

I'd tossed the water bottle in the trash and spent my practice annoyed and thirsty.

After that, I did my best to stay away from Pierce, even if ignoring him completely was impossible. It wasn't enough that he was popular at school and the local ice arenas, but a few news outlets had grabbed hold of his YouTube channel, mostly his greatest hockey hits and the video equivalent of selfies, and turned him into a web celeb. A few professional teams were already showing interest in him. A model-perfect guy with endless charm and enough talent to attract the scouts could rule the world. Or at least his corner of the world, which was unfortunate, because it was a corner of the world I was apparently destined to share.

As Mr. Kozlov finished the final pass over the ice, I skated over to the Zamboni bay. "You didn't mean Pierce Miller, did you?" I asked as soon as he cut off the engine.

Mr. Kozlov started shoveling away the small pile of ice the machine left behind. "Yes! Champion figure skater, champion hockey player, perfect team to teach future Olympians."

Oh no. "You marketed it that way, didn't you? That's how you got the numbers from five to twenty-two?"

Mr. Kozlov set the shovel aside and smiled at me. He had definitely taken a puck or two to the nose when he was younger, if the curvature was any indication. But his smile was straight and wide. "Perhaps." He started closing the Zamboni bay doors.

"I'm not a figure-skating champion."

"Local champion. Regional champion. Champion."

Mr. Kozlov closed the other door and started walking around the outside of the ice. I followed along, letting my skates slide effortlessly across the smooth surface. I raised my voice a little so he could hear me over the rink's half wall. "Not at senior level. Not at nationals. Not a champion that counts."

Mr. Kozlov stopped walking, reached over, and pointed at me, pressing one finger hard enough against the glass to turn his finger completely white. "The Lia Bailey, you count. Senior or national or not. You count."

My cheeks warmed. He believed in me more than I believed in myself. Mr. Kozlov continued walking, and I glanced up at the clock on the scoreboard. Several of the tiny round bulbs were burned out, but it was clearly nine forty-five. Fifteen minutes before the workshop was scheduled to start. I reached the rink's exit and slipped on my blade guards before stepping off the ice. "Can't I just teach the workshop by myself?"

Mr. Kozlov handed me a clipboard with some papers and a pen. "What is wrong with Pierce Miller?"

I bit back the "he's an arrogant jerk who will be a terrible influence on anyone under the age of ten" response that wanted to roll off my tongue. "Nothing. I just think I could do a better job on my own."

An abandoned water bottle lay on one of the benches near the bleachers. Mr. Kozlov deposited it in the garbage can. "He is best hockey player at this rink. Best to teach kids' hockey."

"I know," I said, because it was true. Pierce *was* the best candidate. But that still didn't mean I wanted to teach with him. "It's just that he…he's not…"

"Ah," Mr. Kozlov said. "You don't like him."

If I said yes, I would sound immature, like I was in first grade and Pierce had cooties. I wasn't altogether sure that he *didn't* have cooties, but I shook my head. "I just don't know how well he's going to do with kids." The smooth cover was also true. Mr. Kozlov would have to listen to that.

Instead, he patted my shoulder. "Pierce will be fine. Give him a chance."

I glanced up at the clock again. There was a chance he wouldn't even show up. That would be like him. But as appealing as that possibility was, I'd have to handle all twenty-two kids on my own. My knees wobbled at the thought.

When the doors to the arena lobby swung open to reveal a tiny girl with her mom carrying the world's tiniest, most adorable figure skates, I clutched my clipboard.

Never in a million years did I think I'd say it, but I *needed* Pierce Miller.

Even though it was cold in the rink, sweat was beading on the back of my neck. Pierce hadn't shown up, but all twenty-two of the kids had. Twenty-one of them were currently lined up against the wall, waiting for the workshop to start. However, I couldn't get started because the twenty-second child, a tiny five-year-old named Olivia, would not stop crying.

Olivia had weak ankles and seemingly zero balance. She'd

fallen the second her blades hit the ice. She fell again while trying to get up. She fell while holding onto the wall. She fell while moving. She fell while standing still.

And each time she fell, she cried a little harder.

Now, I was holding Olivia up on the ice on her wobbly ankles and trying to soothe her. The little girl wasn't injured, just frustrated. If I let her get off the ice now, chances were good she'd never step back onto it again. If the tears would stop for just a few minutes, I would be able to help get her feet under her and we could go from there. But either one of those tasks would take individual attention I didn't have time to give.

"Olivia, please stop crying and I'll help you, okay? I'm not going to let go until you're ready, but you have to stop crying so I can talk to the other kids."

Apparently Olivia interpreted this to mean "scream at the top of your lungs." I was about to resort to bribery in the form of candy from the snack bar when another skater hopped on the ice from the far door. I glanced up and relief flooded my limbs.

Pierce was here after all.

"Sorry I'm late." He skated over and came to a hockey stop just a foot or two away from me, sending a spray of ice shavings everywhere. All over me. All over Olivia. All over the closest four or five kids on the wall. He brushed a few of them off, seemingly unsure of what to do with his hands when he got to me. "Er…sorry."

"Whoa," one of the older kids said. "I want to learn how to do *that*."

Olivia stopped crying. Twenty-one jaws dropped open, but mine wasn't one of them. No, I was too busy gawking. You'd think I'd never seen him before, but whoa. Pierce was *hot*. Possibly hotter than the last time I'd seen him. Tall with light brown hair and a body that showed just how much he worked out. Hazel eyes with more green than brown. Something about his jaw made him seem older than he actually was.

But then he had to use that jaw to open his mouth.

"It's Mia, right?"

Four years at the same school and the same rink and he could only get 66 percent of the letters in my name correct? "Lia. With an L."

Olivia started whimpering, so I hushed her in what I hoped was a soothing way.

"Lia," Pierce echoed. He didn't bother introducing himself, as if *everyone* knew who he was. Which they did, but still.

"You're Pierce Miller," said one of the older boys who was wearing a hockey helmet way too big for his head. "My dad says you're going to play for the Red Wings."

Pierce turned toward the row of young skaters, as if noticing them for the first time. "I hope so, little man."

"I saw you on YouTube!" one of the girls said. Though her outfit was predominately pink, she was wearing a tiny pair of hockey skates.

I was so distracted by the kids' hero-worship that Olivia slipped out of my grasp, fell, and started crying again.

"I'm sorry, Olivia," I said as I picked the little girl up and struggled to set her on her skate blades again. The muscles in my back were starting to protest being stooped over for so long.

"I want to skate!" one of the kids said.

"Yeah," another echoed.

The start of a riot. Crap. Like it or not, I was going to have to ask Pierce for help. "Look, you can either take her," I said, nodding to Olivia, "or — "

Before I could finish the other option, Pierce scooped Olivia up and settled her against his hip, her skates hanging down toward his knees. Instantly, her tears stopped.

"Olivia, is it?" Pierce asked. "'Atta girl. You're okay."

That wasn't what I had wanted him to do. Picking her up was just as bad as taking her off the ice. Now he wouldn't be able to put her down, and when he did, she'd just fall or start crying again. But there was nothing I could do about that now, and I had the rest of the kids to worry about.

"Okay, everyone. I want you to let go of the wall and step out in front of you, just like you're walking," I said. One of the kids fell and knocked two others down, but the rest stayed on their feet. "Good job, guys! Now pick up your feet, one at a time."

The kids went back and forth across the rink like that, sometimes falling, always crashing into the hockey boards both because they didn't know how to stop and because it was hilarious enough to cause a fit of laughter every single time. Once they mastered walking, they started pushing off with each foot and gliding, picking up a little speed. I grabbed push bars for the few kids who fell the most, but the others seemed okay.

Every once in a while, I glanced over at Pierce and Olivia. He carried her in his arms for a few minutes, and then put her back down on the ice with his hands supporting her under her armpits. Surprisingly, there were no tears. He skated around the rink with her like that for a while. I got distracted while trying to teach the kids forward swizzles, and the next time I looked over, Olivia was on her own; still weak-ankled and wobbly, but not falling. Even better, she was smiling.

Not that Pierce would have noticed. Now that his hands were free, his phone was out of his pocket, and he was frantically typing something with his thumbs. He was smiling, too.

Texting a girl, maybe?

"Straight to the Olympics with this one," he said without looking up from his phone as they skated by me and the rest of the group.

"I want to go to the Olympics!" one of the little girls yelled right before falling on her butt.

"Me too," another girl said before tripping over the first.

"Okay, okay." I helped both of them back to their feet. "Swizzles first. Olympics second." And apparently not at all if Pierce was their teacher. But I kept that comment to myself. I glanced up at the clock on the scoreboard. Not nearly enough time had passed. I was already more exhausted than if I'd run a long program full-out four times in a row.

It was going to be a long ten weeks.

Chapter Two

PIERCE

I breathed a sigh of relief when the clock changed over to eleven o'clock and Lia called the skaters over to dismiss them.

"Good skating today," Lia said to the kids. "But it's time to go home now."

There were a few complaints from kids who didn't want to leave.

"Yeah, good job," I echoed. Though I hadn't done much more than help Olivia, the kids had still learned a lot. Lia was a natural. Mr. Kozlov had done a good job choosing her to teach.

The crazy old guy was like a second father to me. When I was younger and my dad's company laid him off with no notice, Mr. Kozlov not only gave me ice and hockey time for free, but he'd also hired Dad to help out around the rink until he found a new job. Looking back, I wasn't sure if Mr. Kozlov really needed the help or just knew our family needed the money. Either way, I was grateful. So when Mr. Kozlov asked me to teach a workshop and get some business back into the rink, I said yes without giving it a second thought.

Without looking at my hockey schedule to see that it started the same day as my first game with USA Hockey's U18 National Team Development Program.

Not only had I shown up to the workshop late—not that helping my mom with my brother was anything I could predict or control—I was going to have to leave early. Texting my mom to check on Carson in the middle of the workshop probably hadn't won me Teacher of the Year, either. I convinced myself I'd do better the second week.

"I gotta run," I said to Lia. "Have to get ready for my game." I nodded to the throng of parents waiting to pick up their little skaters. "You got this, right?"

She glanced over at me and brushed a few strands of hair back from her face. When I'd first arrived, her blond hair had been in a tight, neat bun, but throughout the workshop, some of it had escaped. It was prettier this way, but I had a feeling she'd smack me if I told her so. Especially with the look she was giving me now.

"Yeah. I got this," she said in a flat voice.

Crap. "Okay. So...I guess I'll see you next week." I pushed off toward the far door where parents wouldn't be blocking my exit. In a hockey rink, crowds meant people wanting to talk and get autographs. No time for that.

"Pierce, wait!" Olivia called. The tiny thing wobbled her way over to me and threw her arms around my knee. "Thank you for helping me."

A warm feeling worked its way through my veins despite the cold air. That little hug was worth the time away from game prep. I ruffled her hair. "No problem, kiddo. Keep up the good work."

Then I skated off the ice, putting Lia and the kids behind me, and the first game of the season front and center.

Coach tapped the top of my helmet. I barely heard or felt it.

"Make it a good shot," Coach said.

I nodded and headed off the bench. The ice was a mess after three scoreless periods and two scoreless overtimes, but I skated around anyway, tuning out the crowd and gathering my thoughts. The game should have been over by now. I'd had two botched shots during the second period, both of which should have gone in the net. Coach had benched me for the remainder of second period and part of the third, cutting my time in the game much shorter than I wanted it to be. But when it came to a shootout, I was the obvious choice. On the under seventeen team, I'd never missed a shootout shot, and there had been several of them. That percentage was practically unheard of and also the reason why I was third in the shootout lineup.

Bloomington Thunder had made both shots in the first two rounds. We had made one and missed one. If I made the shot, we'd tie it up and go to another round. If I missed, the game was over. The under seventeen team last year had been undefeated. The under eighteen team couldn't start the season with a loss. We wouldn't.

I skated to the center of the rink, where the referee had dropped the puck. The ref checked with the goalie, then nodded to me. "Take your shot."

In that moment, the rink went still and quiet. I wasn't sure if the fans were holding their breath, or if I'd just blocked out the sound. I tapped the puck with my stick and took off toward the net. I picked up speed. Being timid wouldn't get me the point. The goalie backed up toward the net, blocking as much of it as he could, glove and pads ready to stop the puck. For a split second, my mind went to the NHL scouts in the crowd. I'd spotted them during the first period; the premium seats, clipboards, and cameras made it obvious who they were.

I wound up, saw an opportunity to the goalie's right, and took my shot.

Instantly, cheers filled the arena. It took me a minute to realize what was wrong. The cheers weren't from NTDP families and fans. They were from Bloomington Thunder. I had misread the goalie. The goalie had gone to his right. I had shot the puck directly at him, making for an easy stop. We'd lost the game.

The goalie skated over to join his team's celebration, but I stood frozen in place. I looked up at the scouts who were packing up their belongings, no doubt leaving with a terrible impression of my team and me.

"Miller," Coach Tucker called. The teams were shaking hands. I skated over to join them but was so numb I barely felt the other hands against mine. When we finished, I skated over to Coach, my stomach in a regret-filled knot. My teammates pounded me on the shoulders as I passed. The shootout felt so individual, but we'd played as a team and lost as a team. But when I got to Coach, the disappointment was clear on his face. "That goalie's good," he said, with a shrug. "We'll watch the video. See if there's anything you could have done differently. You'll get 'em next time."

He didn't sound any more confident than I felt.

My parents always knew to leave me alone after a loss, especially a painful loss like the one tonight. When I got home from the rink, I went straight to my room to sulk and throw things a little harder than necessary and beat myself up over the fact that I totally screwed up.

Carson, however, did not understand nor care that his older brother needed to be left alone for a while. He knocked on my door because that was the rule, but didn't wait for a response before barging in and tossing himself onto the bed. With tears in his eyes and a pathetic sniffle, he grabbed the silky edge of my blanket and started rubbing it between his thumb and pointer finger.

I turned down the volume on the angry music I'd been playing. Carson took precedence over self-pity. "What's wrong, Bub?"

"Mom's making me eat chicken." The words carried the weight of Carson's ten-year-old world.

Chicken had been okay for a long time, but something about a chicken sandwich from the school cafeteria a few days ago completely ruined that. Mom must have forgotten about the incident.

"Tough night," I said. It was for both of us, just in very different ways.

"Yeah."

"What else is for dinner?"

Carson switched to rubbing the blanket with his other hand. "Salad and noodles."

For Carson, "salad" was iceberg lettuce and ranch dressing, and "noodles" was elbow macaroni with the tiniest bit of butter to keep them from drying out. From my vantage point at the head of the bed, I could almost see Carson's ribs through his shirt. Too many foods were a problem lately, and salad and noodles wouldn't cut it. I set my laptop aside and sat up. "Okay. Let's go."

Carson sat up and wiped the last of his tears away with the back of his hand. "You'll tell Mom no more chicken?"

"We'll work something out," I promised as I followed my brother out of the room. I tousled the back of Carson's hair, which was the same light brown as mine, but poker straight and much too long. "You need a haircut."

Carson bounded down the first few stairs. "It's not in my

eyes yet." He couldn't handle haircuts—something about the sound of the blades against the thin strands or the feel of the cold metal on his neck, or maybe both—so our parents had made a deal that he didn't have to get it cut until it was hanging in his eyes.

"If you say so." When we reached the kitchen, our parents were clearing away their dinner plates while Carson's sat untouched. Clearly there had been a lengthy battle before Carson went for back up.

Mom set her plate down on the counter before reaching up to cup her hand soothingly around my cheek. There was sympathy in her eyes and a wrinkle in her forehead. For a mom, she was pretty in the way that made my friends want to hang out at my house, which always grossed me out. "Hey," she said softly. "You okay?" It was the first acknowledgement of the game and the loss.

"I'm fine," I said, even though I wasn't.

"Unlucky," Dad said. He turned on the coffeemaker for his traditional post-dinner cup of decaf. "Don't beat yourself up over it."

I toyed with the pair of noise-canceling headphones that allowed Carson to attend my games despite the loud crowds and buzzers. They'd been abandoned on the counter in their usual spot, where they would stay until the next game. Not that I was ready to think about *that* yet. "I don't want to talk about it," I said. "I've come to talk about chicken."

"There's nothing wrong with the chicken," Dad said. "It doesn't have sauce on it and it isn't touching the noodles."

Of the three of us, Dad had the least amount of patience for Carson's sensory issues. He just didn't get it.

"It's gross!" Carson said.

Mom rinsed her plate. "I thought chicken was okay."

"It was okay until Wednesday," I said.

She paused, plate halfway between the sink and the

dishwasher. "Oh, right. Wednesday. The cafeteria chicken. I completely forgot."

"I can't eat chicken," Carson said, almost a whimper.

"You can," Dad said. "You just won't. There's a difference."

Mom snapped a towel against her husband's hip. "Brian. Not helping."

I leaned back against the counter and folded my arms over my chest. I tipped my chin up toward Carson. "What do you want to eat?"

"Pizza!"

I should have guessed. Pizza was Carson's favorite food, as long as it was a particular personal-sized frozen brand with the crust that wasn't too thin or too thick and the only topping was cheese. He'd eat it three meals a day all year long if we let him. "Okay. Here's the deal. I put the chicken on a pizza —"

"Pierce, no!" Carson looked completely betrayed.

I held up a hand to stop the protest. "Hear me out. I'll cut it up into tiny pieces and mix it in with extra cheese so you won't even know it's there. But you have to have some cucumber in your salad too, and eat all of it."

Carson considered for a minute. We all held our breath. "Green pepper instead of cucumber?"

"Sold." We shook on it. I may have lost the hockey game, but I won this battle. I grabbed Carson's plate in one hand and a pizza from the freezer in the other. Then I set about cutting chicken into pieces so small it was almost unrecognizable.

"Thank you," Mom said. She pulled a green pepper out of the fridge to help. "We tried bargaining with him, but you have the magic touch."

I shrugged. "He's too skinny. Gotta get him to eat something."

"Speaking of, there's a plate for you in the fridge whenever you're hungry. Chicken and vegetables."

"Thanks."

"Welcome."

"Hey, how was that skating lesson for Mr. Kozlov this morning?" Dad asked, taking a sip from his mug and wincing when it was too hot.

I stuck the pizza in the microwave and grabbed the shredded mozzarella out of the fridge. "It was fine. He got this girl to teach it, and she did most of the work."

"A girl, huh?" Dad asked, the suggestively raised eyebrows evident in his tone. "What girl? A figure skater?"

"Yeah, but not my type. Too…" I trailed off because I didn't know how to finish that statement. "Too something."

"How many kids were there?" Mom asked.

"I don't know, maybe fifteen?"

"Good," she said. "I hope it helps. Mr. Kozlov needs more business."

The microwave beeped. "Pizza!" Carson yelled.

"You're going to turn into a pizza," I said.

"Better than turning into a chicken!" he said back.

I laughed. "True story." I added the chicken and a little more cheese to the top of the pizza before putting it back in the microwave for a few seconds. When I put the pizza in front of my brother, he was already eating his salad, green peppers and all. It was a good sign.

"Thank your brother," Mom said.

Carson did as he was told and blew on the pizza to help it cool.

"You're welcome, Bub."

"Pierce?" Carson said.

"Yeah?"

"I'm sorry you lost your hockey game. You're still the best big brother."

I smiled and ruffled my brother's too-long hair. "Thanks. And you're still the second best little brother."

Carson wrinkled his nose. "But I'm your only little

brother!"

I face-palmed. "Oh, right. Okay. You can be first best then."

He smiled before taking a bite of pizza.

Success, at least in one area of my life.

Chapter Three

That night, I found myself Googling Pierce Miller. What did everyone see in him? I couldn't be the only one who'd had infuriating interactions with him. The first few results were his social media accounts, with thousands of followers and almost as many shirtless selfies. No thank you. Halfway down the page was a link to the USA Hockey website. When I clicked, I landed on the National Team Development Program's fan forum. Most of the posts were from fans, but some were from the players, which I quickly realized were marked with little USA Hockey jerseys next to their usernames.

The first few posts were all about today's game. The under eighteen team had lost in a shootout. A missed shot from Pierce himself had ended the game. Maybe that would be enough to take his ego down a notch or two.

I clicked on a video clip of the shootout someone had uploaded. In the first round, both players made their shots. In the second round, the opposing team made the shot, but

NTDP missed theirs. It was up to Pierce. He skated around for a second before heading over to the ref and grabbing the puck. Then he took off toward the net. Pierce went left at the exact same time the goalie went right. There was no way that puck was making it into the net. Sure enough, it didn't.

There were only a handful of comments on the post with the video. "Unlucky," the first two fans said. The next comment complained about how shootouts turned hockey from a game of skill into a game of chance. What most hockey fans didn't know was that a shootout wasn't chance or luck.

But most hockey fans hadn't had a dad who played in the National Hockey League.

My dad taught me that it wasn't fifty-fifty with the goalie going left or right. There were signs. Signals. If the shooter could accurately read those, the odds were much better than fifty-fifty. My dad's percentage had been much higher than that.

I clicked back to the part of the clip where Pierce's shot started. I waited until he was almost to the net, and then clicked pause. Even from the angle of this amateur video, it was obvious. The goalie's foot was pointing to his right. His weight was back and to the left, like he was ready to push off. The goalie was going right. If Pierce had shot to the goalie's left, he would have caught him off-guard, and the puck probably would have gone in the net.

I clicked back and watched the clip again, and then a third time just to make sure I was right. Each time, I came to the same conclusion. I toyed with the necklace I was wearing. Losing the game might have knocked Mr. Ego down a peg, but he still had about thirty-nine pegs to go, and I had to teach with him for the next nine weeks. A comment pointing out his flaw might just do the trick.

Dropping the pendant back against my neck, I clicked on the "Comment" button. Anonymous or guest comments were disabled, so I had to make an account. A small price to pay for the potential reward. On the account creation page, I used all bogus information.

First Name: Jane

Last Name: Doe

Username: Superfan01 (because I wanted it to be ironic, but both "Superfan" and "Superfan1" were taken)

The only correct information I gave was the fact that I was female and my birth year. I also gave an accurate email address, in case they needed me to authenticate the account. But I set the email address to private so no one else could see it.

With just a few more clicks, agreeing to terms and conditions and the privacy policy, I was an official NTDP forum member. There were places to add information and a picture, but I ignored those, leaving my picture the "Guess Who" type silhouette with the blue question mark. I navigated back to the shootout clip, clicked "Comment," and poised my fingers over the keyboard.

A surge of adrenaline rushed through my veins. I felt powerful that I either saw or knew more than these other fans. That I saw more than Pierce. If he'd seen what I saw, the puck would have been in the net. But he hadn't seen it. So it was only right that I point it out to him.

Check the clip starting at four forty-two. The goalie's skate was pointing right. His weight was set back and to the left, meaning he was going right. Miller should have gone to the goalie's left. Not so unlucky after all.

I let the arrow hover over the "Submit" button. There was a chance Pierce wouldn't even see the comment. But he seemed like the kind of guy who would Google himself or read every comment to find mentions of him. And even if that were true, he'd never have to know the comment came from me. I'd never have to comment again. Just this once. I clicked.

The comment appeared, the lone piece of criticism in a sea of support. But at least it was constructive criticism. That had to count for something. Given all of the non-constructive ways I could have criticized Pierce today, I was really doing him a favor.

"Tell me everything," Embry said as she flopped down on the couch next to me.

A few pieces of popcorn spilled out of the bowl with the motion. I scooped them up before they could leave a buttery stain on the cushion and popped them into my mouth. They burned my tongue, and I swallowed as quickly as I could without choking. "Ouch, that's hot."

"That's what happens when you microwave things for three minutes." Embry removed a piece from the bowl and blew on it before popping it in her own mouth. "Come on. Tell me. Don't you dare leave out any details."

"I thought we were going to watch a movie." It was how Embry and I spent most Saturday nights, either at the theater or watching something on demand. Minus a few holidays and vacations, the tradition had stood since sometime during the fall of our freshman year.

"We were, but that was before you mentioned Pierce Miller. Spill."

I groaned. While discussing movie plans, I'd accidentally let it slip that I'd spent the morning teaching with Pierce. Embry, like most other girls on the planet, thought Pierce was a god: everything from perfect looks to the whole "walking on water" thing. The problem was, my friend had never had enough interactions with him at school to know that he wasn't as much a god as a devil. "He showed up late and played on his phone the entire time, leaving me to deal with twenty-two kids by myself, and then left before they were even dismissed."

Embry sighed. "Come on. I'm sure it wasn't that bad."

"Oh, it was."

"How did he look? What was he wearing? What did he smell like?"

I rolled my eyes at the pure crush status of the questions. "He was wearing hockey skates."

Embry stuck her tongue out and threw a piece of popcorn at me. It landed on my shirt, near my belly button. "Not what I meant." But then she sat up and leaned forward, spilling more popcorn on the couch. "Wait, was that *all* he was wearing?"

I picked the popcorn off my shirt and threw it back. The piece stood out against Embry's long black hair. "No! Are you kidding me? There were kids around!"

Embry shrugged and shook the popcorn to the ground. "After Robbie's party last year, you never know."

Pierce's best friend had a party last year that involved a keg and skinny-dipping. We waited a long time for video or photographic evidence to appear. It never did, which was probably why it became a legend.

"Well today he had clothes on. Jeans, I think. And a USA Hockey sweatshirt."

"Was it the blue one? He looks so good in the blue one."

"You think he looks good in everything."

"Or nothing," she countered.

"Can we talk about something else? You're making me lose my popcorn appetite."

Thankfully, my brother chose that moment to come downstairs. "Hey, Adam," I said. Though my brother and I did not get along, I was happy for the distraction from the current conversation.

"Hey," he said, pulling on a pair of shoes.

"Where do you think you're going?" I asked.

"Movies. I'm walking to Miquela's house. Her mom is

going to drive us."

Okay, maybe the conversation about Pierce was easier than this. "Um, no she's not. You're grounded."

Adam looked up at me. We had the same poker straight blond hair as our mom. "I'll be home before Mom gets home from work."

"Not the point. Grounding means you don't leave, not that she doesn't *know* you leave." At age fifteen, Adam had already been grounded more than I had in my life, which was pretty much never.

"Whatever," he mumbled heading to the front door.

I picked up my cell phone. "I'll call Uncle Drew." Uncle Drew was my dad's brother. They'd played hockey together from the time they could walk, through high school. Even though Uncle Drew didn't have kids of his own, he'd always been a big part of our lives, and even more so after our dad died. When Mom was at work, he was in charge, and I wasn't afraid to call in the troops.

Adam froze with his hand on the doorknob. "Seriously, Lia? How much trouble can I get in at a movie theater?"

I probably didn't want to know the answer to that question. "Upstairs or I call."

He mumbled a string of obscenities and headed upstairs, stomping his feet the whole way.

I set the phone down and sighed. "Sorry about that."

"Man, remember when he was still little and sweet?" Embry asked.

"Barely." Adam had been like this, obstinate and troublesome and mean, for almost as long as I could remember. I worried he was going to get a lot worse before he got better.

Embry tucked her hair behind her ear. "Okay, so last Pierce question. I promise. Did he at least show the kids some good hockey skating?"

"Not really. When he wasn't on his phone, I had him help this one little girl who wouldn't stop crying. Never mind the fact that I had the twenty-one other kids. One was all he could handle."

Embry crossed both hands over her heart. "Oh my gosh, he helped a little girl who was crying? So sweet, I think I just developed diabetes."

"Oh, look. The TV is on." I grabbed the remote and made my statement true.

"Fine. Don't allow me to live vicariously through you. You don't care about me at all. I understand."

I sighed as I headed over to the on demand section. "Do you want to teach with him next weekend? Because I really don't want to. I'd be happy for you to take my place."

"Um, do you remember the last time we went skating? I didn't let go of the wall and still managed to fall twice. All of the parents would demand their money back immediately." Embry tucked one leg up underneath her. She was petite like me and had the body to be a figure skater, but definitely lacked in the skill department.

"Fine. But if I have to keep teaching with him, you can expect complaining for the next nine weeks."

"I look forward to it." Embry turned to the TV for a second, but then turned back to me. "Hey, maybe you should give him a chance? Maybe he'll prove you wrong."

"Maybe," I said, just to put an end to the conversation. But I seriously doubted it.

Chapter Four

After dinner, I set a water bottle on my nightstand and leaned a few pillows against the headboard before flopping down and grabbing my laptop and phone. There was a text on the phone screen.

> Robbie: *tough break, man. No way you could've made that shot. Get 'em next time.*

For just a second, I let myself wish I'd stayed on Troy Preparatory Academy's team with Robbie. The pressure and expectations were so much lower. But then again, so were the potential rewards. I thumbed out a response.

> Me: *Thanks.*

> Robbie: *Not beating yourself up over this are you?*

Robbie: *Because I'll come over and kick your ass.*

I smiled. Robbie and I had played on the same teams from when we were five until last year when I left the school team. He knew my tendency to overanalyze every mistake, especially the big ones.

Me: *Nah, I'm good.*

Robbie: *Liar. You're crying into your pillow.*

That was the thing Robbie and Carson had in common: their ability to make me smile or laugh no matter how upset or pissed off I was.

Me: *Like a girl.*

Robbie: *Knew it.*

I dropped my phone on the blankets. Bracing myself, I headed over to the NTDP forums. I knew I shouldn't look. The forum was a double-edge sword. I loved seeing fans' excitement and praise when the team did well, but those same fans weren't afraid to speak their minds when we did not-so-well. But I knew how badly I'd played, and now I needed to see how badly they'd reacted. I couldn't help it.

There were several posts about the game. Most focused on how great Bloomington played, that NTDP didn't have a chance, but there were a few that commented on the sloppiness I had felt, somewhat from my teammates but mostly from myself.

Coach warned us not to engage in "negative contact" with others on the forum or we'd risk sitting the bench, so I just thanked a few fans that wrote encouraging messages. When I finished, my mouse hovered over a video clip someone had posted of the shootout. Usually I loved watching clips of the games, seeing what I did well, seeing the fans' reactions. But this clip was different. This wouldn't be pretty. I took a deep breath and clicked play.

The first four shots went exactly as I remembered, both teams making shots in the first round, and only Bloomington making it the second round. Then I watched as I skated out onto the ice. Usually I looked calm and collected, like the ice was where I belonged, but my confidence seemed to be gone. I remembered my mind had traveled to the scouts and knew that must have been the reason for it. I watched as I tapped the puck and headed for the net, picking up speed. I shot left. The goalie went right. The puck went straight to him, like I was still in the Pee Wee league. Thankfully, the video stopped after that.

I read through the handful of comments. Most said that I was unlucky. That my perfect shootout streak had to end sometime. But one comment stood out from all the rest. It was longer, and I could tell before reading it that the tone was different. Not as supportive. Instead of just scrolling past it like I'd done with the others, I paused and took the time to read each word.

> Superfan01: *Check the clip starting at four forty-two. The goalie's skate was pointing right. His weight was set back and to the left, meaning he was going right. Miller should have gone to the goalie's left. Not so unlucky after all.*

Immediately, I clicked the clip over to the fourth minute. I squinted at my screen, this time watching the goalie instead of myself. At first I didn't see it. This commenter was crazy. But I pulled the clip back again and paused it right before I took the shot. Sure enough, there it was. Skate pointing right. Weight in a rightward momentum. I had missed the signs. I'd misread the goalie or not read him at all.

"Shit," I muttered under my breath. An unlucky shot felt bad, but a screwed up shot felt even worse. If Coach saw that, I would be doing wind sprints for the entire next practice.

I clicked on Superfan01's profile. To have that kind of eye, either at the actual game or on the clip from the cell phone camera, took talent. It had to be a scout or maybe a coach. Someone trained to look for the little details. But Superfan01's birth year was the same as mine. Not a scout or a coach. And the gender was listed as female. I wondered if I knew her. There wasn't any other information: no picture or other details. Her name was listed as Jane Doe, which couldn't be real.

I clicked on "Jane's" recent comments and posts and found that the shot comment was her first one. Whoever this was, she wanted to get under my skin. Coach's "no negative contact" policy echoed through my mind as I clicked to reply. I could tell her she was wrong. I could defend myself and say that it was easy to see those details on a video you could pause and rewind, but impossible while wearing a helmet and skating toward the net. But as my fingers hovered over the keyboard, I knew neither of those statements was true. I'd messed up. The magic I'd had every time I hit the ice for the past few years hadn't been there. Maybe I got too confident or maybe everyone else's skills were finally catching up to me. Either way, it wasn't good, and Superfan01 seemed to know that.

PierceMiller: *Good eye. I might need a shootout lesson from the master.*

Then I clicked "Submit" before I could say anything that might get me in trouble.

I watched the clip twice more, Superfan01's observation becoming more and more apparent each time. Regret settled heavy in the pit of my stomach along with my dinner. It was just one game, but I couldn't shake the feeling that it might be the beginning of the end.

I minimized the forum and headed over to Instagram before I could drive myself too crazy. The picture I'd posted this afternoon, showing off the team's new and improved jersey, had several hundred likes. My social media presence was even stronger than my NTDP presence. Not everyone followed hockey, or even if they did, not everyone knew about the leagues leading up to the NHL. But everyone was on social media. The guys wanted to be me. The girls wanted to date me. The adults wanted me to become successful and famous so they could say "I knew him when…"

As I scanned through comments and social media notifications, it was clear this crowd either didn't know about the loss and the shootout or didn't care. They'd be much more critical of me if I suddenly developed acne or stopped working out than if I started losing games. That was okay. At least if I was failing in one area of life, I could fall back on the other. Not that I didn't *want* to succeed at both.

I glanced at the clock at the corner of my screen. It was only a little after nine o'clock. Curfew wasn't until midnight. Normally, I'd text one of my teammates. Find something to do. An after party to celebrate. But there wasn't much to celebrate tonight. I'd be back to normal tomorrow. For now I clicked over to the Netflix series I'd been marathoning and settled in for a few episodes. I left the NTDP forum website open just in case Superfan01 decided to reply.

Chapter Five

Once Embry left after the movie, I turned on my tablet, which was still on the NTDP forum site. I clicked refresh, and there were three responses to my comment. The last two were from people I didn't know, one saying that I was wrong, there was no way Pierce could have known where the goalie was going to go, and the other was just one word: "wow." The first comment was from none other than Pierce himself.

> PierceMiller: *Good eye. I might need a shootout lesson from the master.*

I couldn't help but smile. Mr. Ego was impressed with my knowledge. I should just leave the page. End the conversation on that note, giving me a leg up for our next workshop, knowing that he wasn't as invincible as he claimed to be. But something about the anonymity of the online forum made me braver than the real world. I had a little confidence. Maybe not quite to Pierce's level, but still. Confident enough to respond in a way I never would have in person.

> Superfan01: *Oh, you couldn't afford a lesson from me.*

Still smiling, I switched apps to check my YouTube subscriptions. I could watch those until I fell asleep. The first video was only half a minute in when an email notification appeared at the top of the screen. A new comment from the NTDP forums. When I followed the provided link, I found that it wasn't just someone. It was Pierce. He must have been up and online late, too.

> PierceMiller: *If you're so good, why did Matthews miss his shot?*

I hadn't really paid close attention to the shots before Pierce's, but that didn't mean I couldn't. I scrolled up to the initial post with the video and found the second round of the shootout. The back of the NTDP player's jersey read "Matthews." I watched closely as Matthews prepared himself and skated toward the net. The set-up looked good. Unlike Pierce, he seemed to read the goalie's signals, but the puck went directly into the glove. Matthews crumbled; the Thunder cheered. I pulled the clip back a few seconds and watched it again twice. His aim was good, but the puck didn't get high enough.

A memory of my dad teaching me how to get the puck off the ice crossed my mind. It was a vivid memory, so it must not have been very long before he died. I remembered him teaching me how to flick my wrist so the puck would leave the ice and travel through the air. I could almost hear him saying that the second the puck hit the stick was only the first half of the shot, and I had to follow through. My dad was stronger than I was, making the puck almost fly through the air, but I still managed to get a little height.

I remembered growing bored after a while and leaving my dad with the stick and puck in favor of toe loops or whatever element I was working on at the time. My dad had always been a little sad that I'd made the decision as a child to wear the pretty skates with the toe picks instead of the ugly hockey skates. He wanted me to follow in his footsteps and taught me more about hockey than any figure skater needed to know, but I hadn't appreciated any of it. I'd seen the lessons as an interruption to my life rather than the opportunity it was. I wished I could go back to those times and spend hours with him teaching me, spending time with me. But it wasn't really a wish because it could never come true.

I gave myself a little shake back to the present. Wrist. Follow-through. I clicked "Reply" and started typing.

Superfan01: *Aim was good, but the puck didn't get high enough. He needed more flick in his wrist. More follow-through. If he could have had both of those and kept his aim, he would have been good. Even another six inches would have been enough.*

I clicked submit but didn't return to my video. I suspected he'd respond. Sure enough, just a minute later another notification popped up. Pierce had private messaged me through the NTDP site.

PierceMiller: *Who ARE you?*

Again, the confident and witty side of me that seemed to come out of nowhere showed up.

Superfan01: *Would you be afraid if I told you I'm one of your opponents?*

PierceMiller: *No, because you'd be lying. Profile says*

you're female.

Crap. I should have lied about that. But the fact that he'd clicked over to my profile gave me a little jolt of adrenaline. Yes, he was a cocky jerk, but he was an insanely popular cocky jerk, and he noticed me. He was paying more attention to me than he had during the workshop this morning or anytime in the past four years combined. It felt like a weird form of success.

My phone buzzed with another notification from the forum, but this comment was from a different member, username SlapShotSteve, saying how right I was about Matthews' shot. Of course. Now that I had Pierce's respect, I'd have everyone's respect. I didn't reply.

Instead, I clicked on Pierce's private message and started typing. But before I could finish my sentence, another message from him appeared. I definitely had his attention.

PierceMiller: *Which league do you play for?*

He thought I was a hockey player. Of course he did. That was much more reasonable than the truth. But I wasn't about to share the truth. So I went with a partial version of the truth and turned the attention back on him, a subject I knew he'd be more than happy to talk about.

Superfan01: *I don't. What's your favorite part about playing hockey?*

PierceMiller: *You don't play for a league? Do you play for a school? Favorite part…breakaways. When you're skating so fast it feels like flying, and it's just you and the goalie. When that puck goes in, you feel like a million bucks.*

I was surprised. I'd expected him to say something about the attention he received, the fans cheering, or at least winning a game. But his answer made it clear he didn't just love the attention, he actually loved the game. Dad used to love breakaways, too. I remembered my mom jumping up out of her seat, screaming and cheering, practically dropping me or my brother, depending on which kid was sitting in her lap at the moment. I knew the effects of a breakaway before I knew what a breakaway was.

Superfan01: *Sounds amazing.*

I almost hit send, but a statement like that wouldn't require a response. It could mean the end to the conversation, and I didn't want that to happen. Not yet. So I kept typing.

Superfan01: *Did you have any breakaways tonight?*

Based on the losing score, I could probably guess, but this would keep him talking.

PierceMiller: *No. Wasn't in most of the second or third periods. You weren't at the game?*

Superfan01: *Nope. Just caught the clip of the shootout. Was it bad?*

What I didn't tell him was that I hadn't watched a hockey game in person in years, and I had no plans to change that in the future.

PierceMiller: *Yeah. Not my best game, as some of the other fans rightfully pointed out.*

I had seen a couple of the negative comments about Pierce's game. They were probably true, and I gave him a lot of credit for not responding to any of them.

We chatted back and forth for a while, about hockey and NTDP and life, but I was careful not to give any information about my identity. If he knew who I really was, he'd lose interest in a heartbeat. The guy couldn't remember my name or who I was, and the fact that I knew about hockey wouldn't make me any more memorable. But for Superfan01, he seemed to gain interest with each message.

My mom knocked on my door before opening it. She was wearing pajamas, glasses had replaced her contacts, and her long blond hair had been pulled back in a messy bun. "Still up?" she asked.

When I looked at the clock on my tablet, I expected it to be around eleven, but it was well after midnight. There was always a minute or two between Pierce's replies, sometimes more, and I guessed those added up pretty quickly. "Yeah. I'll go to bed soon."

Mom nodded to the tablet. "What are you up to?"

Thankfully it was dark enough in the room that Mom probably couldn't see the blush that warmed my cheeks. "Just talking with a friend from school," I said.

"A *friend*, huh?"

"Yes, Mom. Just a friend. And what are *you* doing up so late?"

She lifted one shoulder in a shrug. "Still getting over not working midnights. I'll be used to it in a few days."

Mom was a NICU nurse at the local hospital. She'd worked midnights for the past few years, but with my brother getting into so much trouble at home and school, she was trying a schedule change to see if it helped.

"Good luck with that."

"Thanks. I'm working seven to seven, so I'll see you after that. Adam's still grounded. Call Uncle Drew if he gives you any trouble."

I gave a salute, and Mom closed the door. My stomach jumped when I saw two new messages from Pierce. The first one sent me to a recent YouTube clip he'd posted. I'd claimed none of his videos were serious, and he'd apparently found one to counter my point. Instead of clicking on the clip, I read his next message.

> PierceMiller: *Still there? You probably went to bed. I should do that, too. Practice tomorrow.*

My heart sank in a way that I never thought would be associated with Pierce Miller. I wasn't ready for the night to be over, because it felt like this was an experience that wouldn't be duplicated. It felt too weird and somehow magical for that.

> Superfan01: *Sorry! Got distracted. Good night!*

I still wasn't tired or ready to log off, so I clicked over to the YouTube video. Unlike most of his videos, which were of him and his friends or him and the team—all action and laughter and energy—this one was still, like he'd set his phone on a stand before hitting record. In the video, he talked about mental and developmental health awareness. How important it was to be informed and accepting of others. It seemed like such a weird topic for someone like Pierce. Maybe it was something his agent or the team's publicist asked him to do? I played the video once more before turning off the tablet, setting it on the nightstand, and turning off the light.

In the darkness, I heard the faint sound of music coming from Adam's room. I wondered if he'd fallen asleep with it on or if he was still awake. I also wondered how Pierce Miller had gone from Mr. Ego to PierceMiller, and how I'd gone from Mr. Kozlov's The Lia Bailey to Superfan01. I wasn't quite fan girl status like Embry or the rest of my class, but the online version of Pierce wasn't so bad. It was amazing how things could change.

On Monday morning, I walked into school with Embry and almost immediately walked into a guy who was too busy talking to someone behind him to look where he was going.

"Oof," I grunted.

"Watch it," Embry added, picking up the book she'd dropped.

When the guy turned, it wasn't just a guy. It was Pierce.

"Sorry," Pierce said. "My bad." He started to turn back to whomever he'd been talking with but did a double take, like he couldn't remember who I was or why he knew me.

I waited for him to connect the dots, but if I held my breath that long, my lips would turn blue. "Lia," I said, "from the workshop at the rink?"

Recognition crossed his face. "Oh, right. Lia. You look different." He motioned to my hair, which was straight around my shoulders, not in the bun like it had been on Saturday.

"Yeah." I wanted to add something about how he looked different, too, no sweatshirt or skates, but that would be something Superfan01 would say. Not me. I would shut up and look at the ground and walk away. So that's exactly what I did.

"Um, awkward," Embry said once we were out of earshot.

"Ugh." My cheeks warmed. "He didn't even remember me. We spent an hour teaching together, we've gone to school together for four years and skated at the same rink since we were kids, and he couldn't recognize me without my hair in a bun. He's such an egotistical jerk."

Embry shifted her books to her right arm so she could link her left through mine. "To be fair, you do look a lot different with your hair in a bun. And he did recognize you, he just couldn't remember how he knew you for a minute."

"Can you please stop trying to defend him and take my side?"

We stopped outside the music room where Embry had first period chorus. Chorus was a class we'd never shared over the past four years. While Embry was one of their star soloists, I didn't have a musical bone in my body. I would only sing along to the radio in the car if it was turned up loud enough that I couldn't hear my own voice.

"Oh, right," Embry said. "Pierce is a jerk. An egotistical one."

"Much better. Thank you." I nodded to the music room door. "Your audition is today, right?"

Embry deflated, clutching her books to her stomach. "Just thinking about it makes me want to puke."

"Hey." I nudged my friend's shoulders back so she stood tall. I ran my fingers through her hair, smoothing the long, dark strands. "There's no reason to be nervous. I've heard you belt 'Wait for It' a thousand times. It was practically written for you." I dug through my purse and pulled out a lip stain I'd bought because I loved the color, but it looked so much better on Embry's caramel skin. "Here. Put this on, then go in there and kick some *Hamilton* ass."

Embry smiled and used the camera on her phone as a mirror to apply it. "Thank you."

"You're welcome." I stuck the lip stain back in my purse. "You got this. No puking."

"Unless it's on Pierce Miller."

I laughed and hugged my friend. "Unless that. See you after."

Then I set off to avoid Pierce until Saturday. What had I been thinking, talking to him this weekend? Thank goodness the internet was anonymous. He'd never have to know, and I wouldn't make that mistake again.

Chapter Six

PIERCE

My feet pounded the pavement while the cool air chilled my aching lungs. I had no clue why everything felt so tough lately. The game on Saturday. Practice yesterday. The run today. My diet had been mostly good, plenty of protein and more kale than I wanted to eat in a lifetime. I hadn't missed a workout or practice. As Robbie and I rounded the corner back to my house, I checked my phone. Almost three miles in twenty minutes. That was our average. It wasn't that we were actually doing poorly; it just *felt* bad.

A minute later, my tracking app informed us we had run three miles, and we both slowed to a jog, then a walk. I put both hands on the back of my head, elbows out, breathing hard. "Did that suck for you?"

Robbie wiped his forehead with the back of his arm. "No. My quads are still sore from my last practice, but other than that it was fine."

I dropped my hands to my waist. "Man. Felt terrible to

me."

Robbie checked his phone. "We kept pace. You're still in good shape."

I didn't want to confess that it felt bad mentally, not physically. Like I was off my game. Maybe it hadn't affected my run performance today, but it clearly had on Saturday and again on Sunday if the number of times Coach swore at me was any indication. Once we approached my house, I punched in the code to open the front door. "If you say so."

"Hello?" Mom called.

"Just me and Robbie," I said as we followed her voice into the kitchen.

She was standing at the counter, chopping a cucumber. "Hi, boys. How was your run?"

I opened the fridge and grabbed bottles of water for me and Robbie. I passed one to my friend. "It was good." It wasn't worth it to tell my parents how I felt the past few days. Dad would just tell me to work harder, and Mom had more than enough to handle with Carson. "What's for dinner?"

"Turkey burgers," she said. "Salad for us, French fries for Carson."

I considered. Turkey burgers had been okay with Carson recently, and fries were almost always okay as long as they weren't mushy. "Sounds good."

"Are you staying for dinner, Robbie?" Mom asked. "I can make extra."

Robbie's water bottle was already almost empty. "No, but thanks for the offer. As soon as I get up the energy, I'm going to head home."

"Let me know if you change your mind. How was school today for both of you?" she asked.

"Boring," I said. "So boring that you should probably just let me finish the year with full-time tutoring." Troy Preparatory was flexible enough to work with students like me who had unusual schedules and missed a lot of school, requiring tutors to complete credits. I had started pushing for full-time tutoring as soon as junior year hit, but my parents wanted me to have the "traditional high school experience." They seemed to forget that my situation was anything but a typical high school experience.

"No way," Robbie said after draining the last few sips of water from his bottle. "You are not allowed to leave me alone at that school. How would I survive Brit Lit without you? It's bad enough that you left me alone on the team and leave me alone on your travel days. You don't get to abandon me the rest of the time, too."

Mom put some cherry tomatoes in a colander to rinse them in the sink. "See? Even Robbie is on my side."

"Traitor," I said, taking a swing at Robbie's head with my own empty water bottle.

We'd been friends so long Robbie seemed to know to expect it, and ducked before it could even come close. "Hey, you secure tutoring for me, maybe we'll talk."

"We did talk, back when it was time for NTDP tryouts."

"Mrs. Miller," Robbie said, "can you believe he's still giving me crap about this two years later?"

She shut off the faucet. "No, Robbie, I cannot."

I laughed. "Hey! Quit ganging up on me!"

"Wouldn't have to gang up on you if you'd get it through your brain. You want to spend the next four years playing for the NHL. I want to spend the next four years playing for Western Michigan. Besides, I'm not good enough for NTDP."

I didn't say that I wasn't sure *I* was good enough for NTDP anymore. "I will make an effort to get that through my brain. Even if I don't agree with a word of it."

Robbie pushed off the counter he'd been leaning against and pounded my shoulder. "Good. That's all I ask." He tossed the water bottle in our recycling bin. "See you tomorrow?"

I almost said yes, but then I remembered. "No. Tomorrow's a travel day. We're in Chicago on Wednesday."

Robbie groaned. "Next time just lie to me and tell me you're going to be there, okay?"

"You know, you're kind of clingy since you broke up with Jasmine. Maybe it's time to find another girl?"

Mom gasped over the bag of fries she'd just removed from the freezer. "You broke up with Jasmine?"

I rolled my eyes. "Old news, mom."

"Well it might be old to you, but it's new to me. When did that happen?"

"Technically she broke up with me," Robbie said, holding up his hands in defense. "It happened two weeks ago. And apparently I'm using your son as a replacement."

"That's your mission," I said.

Robbie squinted at me. "Hooking up with you is my mission?"

"No, smart-ass. Your mission by the time I get back from Chicago is to get another girl. That will keep you occupied while I'm gone."

He considered. "I suppose that's doable. But fair is fair. Your mission while you're in Chicago is to play a kick-ass game. And eat a slice of deep dish for me."

"Deal," I said.

But part of that deal felt like a lie.

Chicago was one of those cities that was too close to fly to but an insanely long drive, so the hours stretched out, unlike my cramped legs. That was why we never traveled on a game day. We needed our legs to be fresh, and that was completely impossible after sitting on a bus or a plane. I had homework to do, but no desire to do it. I was supposed to read part of some

Shakespeare play, but that would take quiet and concentration that I didn't have here. Instead, I took advantage of the bus Wi-Fi and headed over to the NTDP forum. There were already predictions and discussions about tomorrow's game. Several of them commented on the fact that I needed to get my head in the game. If only it were that easy.

I clicked around for a while, thanking a few people who wished me and the rest of the team luck. When I was done, I kept clicking. At first, I wasn't sure what I was looking for, but then I realized: I was looking for Superfan01. I was looking for her insight more than anyone else's.

I typed her username into the forum's search bar and clicked over to her profile. The last comment she made was to me before I switched over to private messages. I wished the NTDP forums were like other websites where I could see the last time she'd logged in.

Wanting to test the waters, I opened a new post. It was rare for me to start a new post. Jackson sometimes did. He was a nice guy who reminded me a lot of Robbie, and he loved interacting with the fans. In the "Subject" field, I typed out *Your Best Advice*. In the body of the post, I typed out *What's your best advice for me and the rest of the U18 team as we head up against Chicago tomorrow night?* To anyone else, it probably looked like just a post from one of the players trying to kill time on the bus. Just like many of my random YouTube videos of terrible sing-alongs during lengthy traffic jams. But really, it was a hook to see if Superfan01 would reply. If we could start a conversation again.

I clicked over to check a few new comments on my YouTube channel while I waited for responses to roll in. I was watching a video from a fellow athlete and YouTube star that played for the soccer equivalent of NTDP when the email notifications started coming in.

Some of the comments were positive, about staying

strong on offense because Chicago was notoriously great at defense. I thanked the commenters for those reminders. Some of the comments were negative, about getting my head out of my ass, and containing more foul language than the forum's usage policy allowed. I reported those posts, not because the language bothered me, but because any kids who stumbled onto the forum shouldn't have to see that. I deleted each notification one by one, thinking I wasn't going to get anything from Superfan01. Or not yet, anyway. But then another email appeared. Sure enough, it was from her.

> Superfan01: *They have a game tonight, so they're going to be tired tomorrow. Use that to your advantage. Lots of breakaways and slapshots.*

I smiled, not only because she'd commented, but because she'd remembered what I'd said about my favorite part of hockey, and also taken the time to Google the other team and look for weaknesses that could be used to NTDP's strengths. This girl was something. Whoever she was.

> PierceMiller: *Great advice, superfan01. Thanks. Good to talk with you again.*

> Superfan01: *Good to talk with you, too. In Chicago?*

> PierceMiller: *On the bus right now. Five hours on a bus is too long, and we still have two to go. I'm glad you're here to keep me company.*

Instead of another comment adding to the thread, the next message from Superfan01 came as a PM.

> Superfan01: *What's it like? Being on the bus with a whole team?*

PierceMiller: *Loud. I've got headphones on right now.*
As smelly as you'd think a bus full of guys might be.
Lots of energy, guys laughing and talking and tossing
food and cell phones and a tennis ball between the
rows of seats.

While waiting for her response, I tapped over to Snapchat and searched for a Superfan01. Unsurprisingly there was one, but it appeared to be a guy in his thirties or forties who was a super fan of Star Wars and probably cared little to nothing about hockey. Not the same person. Or at least I hoped not.

"Hey, Miller," someone called over the music playing in my headphones. I looked up and saw Jackson standing there, his own headphones around the back of his neck, tablet in his hand. "Who's Superfan01?"

I winced. Whoever she was, I wasn't ready to share her. "Just this girl," I said. Not enough information to inspire questions, or so I hoped. I shoved my bag off the empty seat next to me so Jackson could sit. The bus driver for this trip tended to hit the brakes like his life depended on it, and I really didn't want my friend and left wing to go through the windshield if the guy decided to stop.

Jackson flopped down on the seat. "This girl, huh? Does she live around here?"

Another message notification popped up. Superfan01 and I were talking about music. I was currently on a rap kick, while she seemed to like more pop, the kind of music the guys and I only listened to for those YouTube videos. But that was okay. Most girls liked that kind of stuff. I could tolerate it. "Not really." Truthfully I had no clue where she lived. Most NTDP fans were local, but some came from different parts of the country. If she were just a hockey fan in general, she could even be from Canada.

"I saw her comment about your shootout shot. She

knows hockey. That's hot. Are you private messaging her? Is she single? Have you seen a picture of her?"

With each question, Jackson leaned a little farther over my screen, trying to get a peek. I shoved him back. "Dude, no." I laughed. "Back off."

"Oh, shit. Is she ugly? Is that why you're being so nice to her? Because you feel bad?"

"No," I said immediately. But it wasn't so much that I knew she wasn't ugly as that I didn't care. There was a first time for everything.

> PierceMiller: *Do you know my teammate Luke Jackson? Number 42? He spotted our conversations and is asking about you.*

> Superfan01: *I don't know Jackson, but tell him I said hey.*

That was surprising. If I was the most popular player on the team, Jackson was next. If she paid close enough attention to NTDP to know about my botched shot, why didn't she know about Jackson? She could have been a follower from my YouTube or Twitter accounts and not into hockey, but she knew way too much for that to be true. Something wasn't adding up.

"Superfan01 says hey," I said.

Jackson looked over and smiled. One of his front teeth was much whiter than the rest. It was probably a fake after taking a puck to the mouth. "Tell her I said hey back. And that I'm single. And also gorgeous."

The bus driver slammed on the brakes, and my tablet went flying. It was a good thing I'd had Jackson sit down. "See, even the bus driver doesn't want me to say that."

"Damn, he needs to have his license taken away. Or the

brake pedal loosened. One of the two."

I grunted in agreement as I picked up my tablet, which was thankfully undamaged.

PierceMiller: *He says hey. I'm not telling you the rest of his response because it's ridiculous. Most of the guys I play with are ridiculous, tbh.*

"Can we just freaking be there already?" I asked as the bus driver slammed on the brakes again.

Jackson leaned forward to get a good look out the window next to me. "Doesn't look like Chicago to me. Not yet."

My stomach twisted. As much as I wanted to blame it on the terrible driving, I knew that wasn't the case. I wanted to be off the bus, but I didn't want to be in Chicago. Chicago meant another game. One I wasn't sure I was ready for. I hoped Superfan01 was right and their players would be tired. I was afraid I was going to need every advantage I could get.

Chapter Seven

LIA

Thursday evening was one of the more rigorous practices with my coach. We focused on jumps, moves in the field, and whatever program I was currently working on. Tonight it was my long program for regionals, set to Beethoven's Moonlight Sonata. The music was dark and somewhat depressing, but I loved it. Something about the repetition, the minor chords, and the clashing notes was beautiful. The version my coach had selected had a small orchestra, not just a piano, which added the depth I needed, especially as I headed into my jumps. The program finished with a spin, and I loved the contrast when my spinning sped up as the piano notes slowed to a close.

When I finished, slightly dizzy and out of breath, I immediately looked over to my coach. Kat Burnette was one of those people who just looked like a figure skater: petite, hair constantly in a bun, too-pink blush on her cheeks and too-red stain on her lips. Usually I could tell with one look at Kat's face whether I'd nailed it or not, but tonight her face was impossible to read. I skated to the boards and slowed through a T-stop.

"How was that?" I asked, slightly breathless. I didn't usually have to ask.

"It was good." Kat's tone didn't match her words.

"It was good, but…" I prompted, waiting for the other skate to drop.

"You should be skating at the senior level."

My stomach clenched. Senior was the highest level in U.S. Figure Skating. It was the level that led to Nationals, Worlds, and the Olympics. "But I just passed the junior test this year!"

"Yeah, and you could pass the senior test, too. You can do all of the required jumps. We added a spiral sequence even though you didn't need it for juniors. We just have to add a double lutz and extend the music by thirty seconds. You've got enough stamina for that."

I dug the heel of my blade into the ice, creating a tiny divot. "I can't."

"Look at me." In addition to coaching on figure skating talent, Kat also coached on poise. Looking at the ground while talking was never an option. When I looked up, Kat smiled. "Much better. Why can't you?"

I had to fight to keep my gaze on Kat's. I wanted to look somewhere else, anywhere else, so Kat wouldn't see the memories and emotions that were currently traveling through my mind. The Olympics had been my dad's dream for me. I remembered when I was little, my dad found these foil-wrapped chocolate disks that looked a lot like medals. He'd taken a gold one, attached it to a ribbon with some glue, and when it dried, draped the "medal" around my neck. I wore that medal so often it melted and got smashed and he had to make another one. "That will be you one day," he'd said while we watched the ladies' medal ceremony when I was eight. "I'll be cheering for you in the stands."

But now his statement would never come true. After he died, I quit skating for a couple of years. I didn't want anything to do with ice arenas. But I finally admitted to the therapist my mom forced me to see that I missed it, and she suggested it might be good to get back to it. Mom didn't push it and certainly didn't say anything about the Olympics, but signed me back up. What I lacked in a couple years of training, I made up for in talent. Jumps and footwork came naturally to me, and spins were mastered with some work and practice. Within a year or two, I'd caught back up to those I'd left behind. Within another year, I'd surpassed them.

But I couldn't imagine making it very far in skating without my dad's support. I couldn't imagine getting anywhere close to that podium without him in the stands, cheering me on. Just thinking about it made me feel sick, and maybe a little guilty. The opportunity for me to accomplish my dreams was still out there. For my dad, the Red Wings won the Stanley Cup the year *after* he died. The team dedicated the win to their former player. There was a blurry newspaper picture of our family with the Stanley Cup—me statue-still, not even smiling, my mom, smiling through her tears and holding Adam, who was still too young to really understand what was happening.

"I'm afraid I won't be good enough." It wasn't a lie. I was terrified of that. It just wasn't the *whole* truth.

Kat's face flushed with excitement under her blush. "But you are! That performance you just gave? With a little polish it would be senior-level ready." Kat leaned over the half-wall to the hockey bench where she always stored her phone and removed one of her giant mittens so she could thumb at the screen. "I think there's a test in a few weeks in Ohio. You'd pass in plenty of time to change your registration for regionals from junior to senior."

"*If* I passed, which I wouldn't because I never agreed to

this plan in the first place."

"I just need to find a version of the song with thirty extra seconds," Kat said, completely ignoring my statement and pounding away at her phone screen. "Aha. Four minutes, one second. Perfect." She reached into the scoreboard area and hooked her phone up to the rink's sound system. "Okay, let's just try it. Keep the ending as-is. Change your second double toe loop to a double lutz. Where there's extra music, just improvise. I'll use that to re-do whatever choreography needs to be re-done."

I glanced up at the clock. "We don't have enough time. There's another practice in here after me."

"Stop making excuses and get out there! We'll finish in plenty of time if you do less talking and more skating!"

I sighed and pushed off the boards, skating to the center of the rink and striking my opening pose. I was exhausted. It had been a long practice with several program run-throughs, and here I was doing it again, but longer this time. I was going to be sore the next day. The music began and I started my footwork. This version of the music was almost the same as the original, just a little slower in some spots. It shouldn't have been enough to throw me off, but I found myself tripping and slipping on dumb things like footwork and three-turns. As much as I wanted to blame it completely on exhaustion, I couldn't, because the words "senior test" wouldn't stop echoing through my mind. I somehow remembered to change the double toe loop to the double lutz, but two-footed the landing. When the extra music appeared, I filled it with some footwork, spirals, and a single axel, but it felt rough. Choppy. Stiff.

Out of the corner of my eye, I caught someone standing by the entrance to the ice. My choreography took me in that direction, and I saw familiar curly light brown hair. Pierce. The fact that he was watching threw me even further off my game.

When I went into a double salchow, I under-rotated and fell hard on my hip.

"Shake it off," Kat called.

I got up quickly and fought to catch up with the music. My cheeks were hot with some combination of exertion, knowing Pierce had just seen me wipe out, and realizing I *cared* that Pierce saw me wipe out. I headed into the spiral sequence and regained a tiny bit of the confidence this program was sucking out of me. Spirals were always my favorite. When I was younger I always thought the name meant they were a spin, but later realized they were the beautiful move in which the skater skated on one leg, the other leg extending as far back and above her as possible, pointing toward the sky. They were simple but not easy, depending on the skater's flexibility. I was very flexible.

I made it through the end of the program without falling again, and took my closing pose. When the music stopped, I heard clapping from Pierce's direction. I ignored it and skated over to Kat, who had one eyebrow raised. "Friends of yours?"

I glanced over at the rink entrance, where Pierce and Robbie Jenkins were waiting to get on the ice. Great. "Just guys from school."

"Don't mumble. Did you hurt yourself on that fall?"

"A bruise. Nothing more," I said, careful to enunciate each syllable. "But that program was terrible. I'm not ready for this."

"It's the end of a long practice. You're tired. It will be just fine next time. I'll work on choreography. You talk to your mom about the senior test. I really think this would be good for you, Lia."

I was about to respond when I heard skates on the ice. I glanced up at the clock. I still had two minutes left in my ice time, but apparently Pierce and Robbie didn't care about that.

Kat leveled a steely glare in their direction. "Excuse me!"

Uh oh. Kat didn't take crap from anyone. Not even Pierce Miller.

"Yeah?" Pierce called from across the rink.

"Kat, it's fine," I said quickly. "It's only two minutes early. I'm exhausted."

Kat completely ignored me. "We're not finished yet. We have two minutes left."

"Oh. Well you were just standing there talking, so we thought you were done," Robbie said.

"We weren't. You need to ask first. That's the polite thing to do."

"Yes, sir," Pierce said, giving a mock salute and then skating off the ice while Robbie snickered.

I sighed. Why did in-person Pierce have to be so much different from online Pierce?

"Are those boys always that disrespectful?" Kat asked.

"No. Usually they're worse."

Kat made a "tsk" sound, then nodded to the now empty ice. "Double salchow. You need to make up for the one you fell on."

I could *kill* Pierce. Kat totally would have let me finish a few minutes early if she weren't so determined to prove a point to Pierce and Robbie. If I fell again, it was their fault. I took to the ice on spent legs, but still managed to pull out two double salchows before the buzzer signaled the official end of my ice time.

"Done now?" I called.

"Yes. Talk to your mom."

Funny, I didn't remember saying "yes" to the whole thing. But I could worry about that later. Right now I needed to worry about the fact that my blade guards were right by Pierce and Robbie. There was no way I could get off the ice without them, but I really didn't want to talk to the guys. I tried to remind myself that somewhere beneath his cocky exterior, this Pierce was the same as PierceMiller, and skated over to the entrance. I opened the door and reached around to grab my blade guards.

"Oh," Pierce said now that I was close enough for him to identify me. "I didn't realize that was…you."

The way he said "you" made it clear he *still* couldn't remember my name. Asshole.

Robbie cleared his throat. "Pierce, aren't you going to introduce me to your friend?"

I looked up from putting on one of my blade guards just in time to see Robbie's waggling eyebrows. Gross. "No, he's not," I said as I slipped the other guard on, "because even though we've gone to school together for four years, skated at this rink together since we were kids, and taught a workshop together, he still can't remember my name."

"Yes, I can!" Pierce said. "You're Lily."

At least he'd gotten the first two letters correct this time. "Lia," I said. Again.

"Lia? Are you sure?"

God, I could *kill* Pierce Miller.

"Ignore him," Robbie said. "So you go to Troy Prep?"

"Yeah. We don't have any classes together."

"Still. Seems like I should have seen you around. Seems like I should have noticed you."

That was the thing. When I wasn't on the ice, I blended in. That was how I liked it. That way, I wasn't the daughter of the Detroit Red Wings' player who'd died after receiving a nasty concussion during game. I wasn't the figure skater who won a bunch of competitions but was too scared to tackle the ones that counted. I was just the short girl with blond hair who kind of kept to myself. If I went to the senior level, some of that anonymity was bound to disappear.

"No, you shouldn't have," I said. "Have a good practice." Then I grabbed my water bottle and walked away.

Chapter Eight

PIERCE

I walked through the front door, dropped my book bag and keys, and headed straight for the couch. When I flopped down on my stomach, the leather was cool against my skin. I closed my eyes. I hadn't slept well, I was skating extra outside of practices, trying to get back in the game, and school had been particularly boring today. The combination was lethal. I sighed and smelled laundry detergent. The house always smelled like Tide on Thursday afternoons. It was probably my most girly feature, but I kind of loved it. I loved the predictability of laundry day.

"No shoes on the couch," Mom said.

With a grunt, I swung my feet to the side so my shoes weren't technically on the couch.

"Hey. You okay?"

I opened one eye. Mom was standing over me, a mildly concerned look on her face. "I'm fine," I said, more to the couch than to her.

"Bad day?"

I grunted. There had been quite a few bad days lately.

Mom tugged my shoes off and deposited them near the door. "Scooch," she said, motioning me away from the spot on the couch that was always hers.

I sat up just long enough for her to sit down, then sprawled on my back, my head resting on her knee. My feet hung over the edge of the couch. It had been a long time since I'd been short enough to fit here.

Mom ran her fingers through my hair. "Spill."

I sighed. "Just a lot of things adding up, I guess. We're losing, I'm playing terribly, and I'm exhausted from trying so hard *not* to play terribly."

"Have you talked to Coach?"

"Yeah. He keeps telling me to get my head in the game. That I haven't lost my talent, I'm just making mental mistakes."

Mom smoothed her hand over my forehead. "That sounds valid. Why do you think that is?"

I shrugged one shoulder against her knee. "The pressure, I guess."

"It's a lot. The attention from the NHL, everyone watching you online… Is it too much?"

"No." I ran a finger over part of the couch where the leather was starting to crack. "I just need to get used to it. And fast." I sighed again. "Have you checked your email lately?"

When she responded, her tone was hesitant. "No. Why, should I?"

"There's an email from my English teacher. I failed a test."

She nudged me up for a second so she could pull her phone out of her pocket. She tapped the screen a few times, then started reading, her lips mouthing the words while she read.

"It was Shakespeare. Have you ever tried reading that

guy's plays? It's like reading a foreign language."

"Did you ask your tutor for help?"

"Yes. She tried acting out a scene of the play with me."

"Did you play Romeo or Juliet?"

"Har, har," I said.

She frowned down at her phone. "I just logged into my parent account. You're failing English. And math."

I squinted up at the back of her phone. I knew I wasn't doing so great in math, but I didn't think I was failing. Then I remembered my last math test, which I had, in fact, done pretty terribly on. "I can submit corrections for my last math test. That will bring the grade up a little."

"On the bright side, you've got an A in Advanced Strength Training."

Physical education classes were about the only grades above a C I ever received. That and grades from teachers who were big hockey fans. Clearly my teachers this year did not fall into that category.

Mom set her phone on the arm of the couch and went back to running her fingers through my hair. It was too long, which meant it was curling more than normal. I'd have to make an appointment for a cut soon. Maybe make one for Carson, too.

"So what are we going to do about this?" she asked.

"I'll ask for some extra credit. Maybe get help during lunch or before school."

"Both good ideas. You know, your dad and I were just talking. Have you thought about which colleges you're going to apply to?"

My defenses shot up fast and hard. "I'm not going to college."

"We know that's not the plan. And you know we're supportive of your dream to play in the NHL. But we also think it's good to have a back-up plan."

Panic clenched at my gut. My parents had never pressured me about college before. As soon as NHL teams started showing interest while I was playing for NTDP's under seventeen team, college went out the window. The NHL was a dream for many players, but for me it was more than that. It was my plan. Dreams didn't always come true, but I had never made a plan that didn't happen. "What are you saying? I'm such a shitty player this year that no one's going to want to draft me next year?"

"Pierce, no. You know that's not what I mean." From down the hall, the dryer buzzed, interrupting our conversation. "Hold that thought. I'll be right back." She stood and I let my head drop back to the couch, weighted down by this new doubt.

When Mom returned, she was carrying a basket full of towels. "Here. Sit up and help me. Folding laundry is good for the soul."

"Lies," I said. "You hate folding laundry and want me to do some of it for you."

"Perhaps. Fold anyway."

I sat up and grabbed a towel from the basket. They were warm and smelled like fabric softener. It was soothing. Maybe Mom was right.

"So," she said, "the thing about the NHL is that a lot of it is outside of your control. The scouts, the other players, the decisions other people are making…you can't do anything about any of that."

I folded a washcloth into fourths and started a stack on the coffee table. "How I play is under my control. I can turn it around. I can work harder." Even as I said the words, they exhausted me. I was already trying so hard.

"I know you can," she said. "But let's face it. You could have a perfect season, and something could go wrong. The scouts could decide they don't want any players whose names start with the letter P or live in Michigan or whatever. The NHL could have a lockout like what happened a few years ago. Not to mention the fact that you could break your leg in six places tomorrow and have to quit for the rest of your life."

"Six? Four or five wouldn't be enough?"

She flicked a washcloth at my knee. "You know what I mean. The NHL is an amazing dream, and it's a dream we think you can accomplish, but we also think it's a good idea to have a back-up plan in place."

"Like college," I said.

"Like college," she echoed.

I tugged on a loose thread at the end of one of the towels. It unraveled even more. As much as I wanted to appease my mom and say I would apply so we could move on, the elephant in the room had to be addressed. "Okay, so say I do decide to apply to a college. My transcript is going to be less than impressive."

"Colleges look at more than just grades. They'll look at extracurriculars as well, which you've clearly got. There are athletic scholarships and some schools right here in Michigan with really good teams."

"And if I apply to those schools and still don't get in?"

"There's always community college. You can go there for a year or two before working your way up to a school with a team."

"No," I said, balling the towel up in my hands. For the first time my future felt questionable. I wasn't a fan of the feeling. "No way. I hate school and I suck at it and the only reason I would even *think* about jumping in to four more years of suffering is if the NHL didn't pan out and I had to play at the university level. No other reason. Not happening. So what then? Should I start practicing 'do you want fries with that' now or later?"

"Okay, okay," Mom said, squeezing my knee. "Calm

down. We're talking worst-worst-worst case scenario here, which probably won't happen, okay? But maybe we should prepare for the worst-case scenario and apply a few places, huh? We can start tonight. I'll help."

I sighed. "Sorry. I'm just frustrated. And exhausted."

"I know you are. That's why I'm offering to help. Besides, maybe having a back-up plan will relieve more of your stress than you realize."

At that moment, the cell phone on the arm of the chair started ringing. Mom glanced at the screen and winced. "The elementary school."

I looked at the clock on our DVR. Getting a call while Carson's school was in session was never a good thing.

"Hello?" Mom held the phone in one hand and continued folding with the other. "Yes it is." She paused mid-fold. "Oh no. I'm so sorry. Yes, of course. I'll be right there to get him. Thank you."

"What happened?" I asked as soon as she hung up.

"Apparently Carson's teacher was dissecting a frog in science class. Carson started melting down, and one of his classmates made fun of him, so Carson punched him in the nose."

Secretly, I was proud of my little brother for standing up for himself. But Mom's expression made it clear that saying so would not be the right thing to do. "Is Carson okay?"

She stood and stuck her phone back in her pocket. "The secretary didn't really say. But you know Carson. Probably not. Ugh, fighting. I thought we had a few more years before there was a possibility of this coming up."

I stood and started putting my shoes back on. "In Carson's defense, he was probably over-stimulated. The smell of formaldehyde alone would be enough to set him off, not to mention the sounds involved."

"You're right." She nodded to my shoes. "Where are you

going?"

"With you. If he's upset, I want to be there for him. I'll worry about colleges and the NHL and folding towels later."

Mom reached up and cupped her hand around my cheek. "That's how I know you're going to be all right. No matter what happens, you're going to be okay because you care so much. About hockey. About others. You're going to be just fine."

I forced a smile and tried to believe her.

After dinner, my parents encouraged me to at least look into a few colleges or universities. I said I would, mostly just to get them off my back. When I flopped down on the couch with my laptop, I did open a browser and typed in one of the local universities. First priority: making sure they had a hockey team. Check. Then I headed over to the undergraduate section and checked admission requirements. My GPA was below the required three-point-two, but above the two-point-five, which could still be accepted after consideration. However, the ACT score requirement was an eighteen. I'd only taken the ACT because they offered it at my school, and anyone who didn't take it had to spend the entire day doing an extra research paper. There was only one thing I hated more than standardized testing, and that was research papers. So I'd taken it and gotten a fifteen. Troy Preparatory offered a couple of additional sessions on Saturdays for people who wanted to re-take the test and improve their scores, but I couldn't be *paid* to sit and take a standardized test all day on a Saturday.

Crossing that school off my list, I checked another. No hockey team. It also got crossed off the list. When I tried one of the larger universities, with an awesome hockey team, the requirements were even stricter than the first school I'd looked at.

It didn't take long to realize that if I didn't get my act together in hockey, I was screwed. I'd end up at a community college with no hockey team, or one that would get me nowhere. When I was little, my friends would change what they wanted to be every single day. One day they'd want to be a police officer. The next, a racecar driver. The next, a doctor. For me the answer had always been the same: a hockey player. And though it was one of those professions that made people look at kids and say, "Oh, it's adorable to have big dreams," no one had ever said that to me. As soon as they saw me play, they knew it could be a reality.

I closed the tabs and headed over to the NTDP forums instead. I hadn't been on much since the last loss. It wasn't pretty. People who, after the first loss, said I should just shake it off, that no one was perfect, and everyone lost sometime, were now harshly critiquing my playing. Saying I was past my prime at the age of seventeen. It was frustrating mostly because I couldn't say anything to defend myself. They were right.

I started scrolling through the posts faster, as if that would make them hurt any less, but paused when I saw Superfan01's name. I clicked on the comment. The post she commented on was short and not so sweet: *Pierce Miller can't turn this around. The U18 team had better find another star before it's too late.*

Superfan01: *He could turn it around. He just doesn't want to.*

Finally, a comment I could say something about because it was so blatantly wrong. I cracked my knuckles and started typing.

Chapter Nine

LIA

When I glanced down at my tablet, there was a message notification from the NTDP forum. I expected it to be from the guy whose post I had commented on, calling Pierce out, but it wasn't. It was from none other than Pierce himself. Good. I was glad he'd seen my comment. I was pissed at him for what he'd said and done during our run-in at practice.

> PierceMiller: *Would I be doing two-a-days and practicing on my own if I didn't want to turn it around? I don't think so. I'm trying.*

> Superfan01: *Try harder.*

> PierceMiller: *Easier said than done.*

I rolled my eyes. He expected everything to be handed to him on silver platter, to be simple and easy, and when it wasn't, he didn't know how to act. He had such a twisted view on reality. I shouldn't be encouraging this conversation. I shouldn't be egging him on. But I couldn't help it.

Superfan01: *If it were easy, everyone would do it.*

Which was quite possibly the most hypocritical thing I'd ever said considering my own issues with skating. I frowned and started typing an apology—

PierceMiller: *You're right. "Easy might be the same as possible, but difficult isn't the same as impossible."*

My breath caught in my chest and I nearly dropped the tablet. It was a quote my dad had said back in an interview, either before I was born or when I was too young to remember. But the quote had gained popularity when he'd died, people sharing pictures of him with that text in front of it. Since then it had gained popularity outside of the hockey world, my dad's words splashed across various social media sites to inspire people of all kinds. Not just hockey players. I liked to think that quote was one of the ways my dad would most want to be remembered. But that didn't make seeing it every time sting any less.

Especially since it also applied to my situation.

Once I got over my surprise at seeing it used now and the wave of memories that came with it, I panicked a little. Did Pierce know that I was Superfan01? Did he somehow know that my dad was Steve Ziegler? My "dad," the hockey player, wasn't actually my father. My father from the biological definition was some deadbeat who hadn't wanted anything to do with me and abandoned us shortly after I was born. My mom met my *dad* when I was one. They hit it off, married quickly, and he'd been the only dad I'd ever known. Since I still had my mom's maiden name, not everyone knew that

Steve had been my dad, and I didn't make a point to change that. Talking about him brought up too many memories, and the looks of either sympathy or horror on their faces made me sick.

But if people who knew me well didn't know Steve was my dad, and if there were a million other people on the earth who could be Superfan01, there was no way Pierce could know. He was a hockey fan. Had been around hockey and the Detroit Red Wings his entire life. He'd probably just heard the quote a thousand times and used it without thinking about it. I took a calming breath and started typing.

Superfan01: *Big Steve Ziegler fan?*

PierceMiller: *The biggest. My favorite. I have a signed jersey of his. Lost one of the greats way too young.*

The anger I'd been feeling toward Pierce melted some. He was more sincere in print than he was in person, and he seemed pretty sincere on this.

Superfan01: *True story.*

PierceMiller: *Do you have a favorite?*

At first, I started to type out the name of the U.S. figure skater that'd won the Olympic medal back when my dad was still alive. But then I realized Pierce meant favorite hockey player, not figure skater. Saying Steve Ziegler would seem like a copycat answer, so I decided to go a different route. After all, I was safe behind my keyboard.

Superfan01: *Well, I would have said you, but…*

I clicked over to Instagram while I waited for him to

respond. Either he was taking longer than normal or I was just anxious for his response, but it felt like forever before the next private message popped up.

PierceMiller: *But you want a player who actually plays well for a team that actually wins? Pssh. So demanding.*

I grinned. Not only was he more sincere in print, but he was also more humble. Self-deprecating. It was cute.

Superfan01: *I know. I ask a lot.*

PierceMiller: *Let me ask you something. Clearly you weren't honest about your name. Were you honest about your gender and age?*

I hesitated with my finger poised over the tablet screen. I didn't want to give too much away, but I also didn't want him to think he was talking to a forty-year-old guy or anything.

Superfan01: *Gender is correct. Birth date is within two months of the one listed. The year is correct.*

While I didn't want him to know who I really was, I kind of liked sharing a tiny bit of information about myself. Of infusing a little bit of who I actually was with the picture he must have of me in his mind.

PierceMiller: *You know, it's kind of not fair. You know so much about me, and I know next to nothing about you. Just that you know hockey, are a chick, and are vaguely the same age as me.*

Superfan01: *What else do you want to know?*

As soon as I clicked "Send," I wished I hadn't. He was certainly going to come back with "What do you look like?" or "What are you wearing?" or something that would piss me off just as much as he had earlier. Sure, I had walked right into it, but I'd still be pissed.

PierceMiller: *If you could change one thing about yourself, what would it be?*

To say I was surprised was an understatement. It was such a deep question, and the complete opposite of what I'd expected. I had to think for a minute or two before typing out a response. I wondered if he was eagerly waiting for my response as I eagerly waited for his.

Superfan01: *I think I'd like to be less afraid. Less afraid of failure. Less afraid of success. Less afraid that some random tragedy is going to strike out of the blue on a Tuesday.*

I had the word "again" at the end of the last sentence, but deleted it. He didn't need to know that a random tragedy *had* struck out of the blue on a Tuesday, and what I was most afraid of was that something similar would happen a second time. Once was more than enough.

PierceMiller: *Interesting. Would you want no fear, or just less than you have now?*

I considered. On one hand, I knew a healthy level of fear kept me from walking on a balcony ledge or walking in downtown Detroit by myself at night. But on the other hand, it would be amazing to be brave. Instead of being afraid to fall, I could be prepared to fly.

Superfan01: *No fear. Screw the consequences.*

PierceMiller: *I don't know, you don't sound very afraid to me…*

Superfan01: *In this hypothetical situation, I am unafraid. Wouldn't that be amazing? Come on, even the great Pierce Miller must have a fear you'd like to get rid of.*

PierceMiller: *Getting rid of the fear of failure wouldn't be so terrible.*

For someone who'd succeeded as much as Pierce already had, fear of failure seemed kind of ridiculous. His life was practically the definition of success.

Superfan01: *Fear of failing at what? Hockey?*

PierceMiller: *Yeah. And other stuff, too. Like school and family stuff and talking to smart, sweet girls.*

Even though I was sitting alone in my bedroom and had no reason to be embarrassed, my cheeks flushed. Was he flirting with me? And not in a gross, "I want to hook up with you" way, but a sweet, honest way? Did Pierce even know what that was or how to do it?

I refused to believe that was possible. If he could, I was in serious trouble.

We continued chatting back and forth for a long time. We talked about serious things like goals and dreams and some not-so-serious things like TV and the fun things he'd done to get in trouble at school lately.

PierceMiller: *Okay, but really, how much would someone have to pay you to go streaking through your school?*

Superfan01: *I don't know…the people at our school can be pretty brutal…probably five million dollars. At least. You?*

There was a pause before his next response. I could almost picture him doing the math. His wouldn't be as high. Enough to buy a car? A new pair of hockey skates? A can of pop?

PierceMiller: *Fifty dollars. But I would have to have the cash up front. And only if no pervy teachers were looking.*

It was about what I expected. Pierce was so used to being in the public eye, he was a lot less shy than I was. But speaking of teachers, the pile of homework sitting on my nightstand was starting to send waves of guilt my way.

I'd never neglected homework, but the NTDP forum and Pierce's messages had totally distracted me in a way nothing had before. Not terrible TV or online shopping or an engrossing book. Maybe I was beginning to understand what all the fuss over Pierce Miller was. The difference was that I understood the fuss over his personality, what was on the inside. I needed to figure out why the Pierce on the forums didn't match the Pierce at school or the rink, and if the two could ever be reconciled. But not tonight.

Superfan01: *Fair enough requirements, even for a ridiculously small amount of money.*

Superfan01: *Hey, this has been fun, but it's getting late, and I still have some homework to do for tomorrow…*

PierceMiller: *Don't let me stand in your way. Good night, Superfan. (For the record, I think you should give me your first name. Just because it feels weird saying good night to Superfan.)*

Superfan01: *Maybe someday I'll let you guess.*

Then I clicked off the tablet and got started on homework with a smile on my face.

When I got to the rink on Saturday morning, I was surprised to see Pierce's car already in the parking lot. On time. Early, even. But it was definitely his car. Not only was it brand new and decked out with giant rims, but it also had an oversized USA Hockey window decal on the back. For a second, I allowed myself to hope that he felt bad about how last week's workshop had gone, and was here early to make up for it. That the virtual Pierce Miller might be rubbing off on the real life one.

When I walked inside the ice arena, the unique combination of the smell of manufactured ice, hockey players, and concession stand popcorn reached my nose. Mr. Kozlov was in the pro shop near the front of the store, sharpening a pair of hockey skates.

"Hello, Mr. Kozlov!" I called. He looked up suddenly and I winced, afraid he might accidentally cut off a finger.

"Good morning, The Lia Bailey! You mold young skaters today! Make them champions."

"I'll do my best," I promised. I adjusted the skate bag on my shoulder and walked to the rink where the workshop would take place. Though it was early, when I opened the door, the lights were already on. I was about to let the door slam behind me when I heard voices. I grabbed the door just in time, something telling me to let it close silently.

"Don't let them get to you. They're probably opponents, trying to get in your head. Make you doubt yourself."

The voice wasn't familiar. Whoever was speaking was blocked from sight by the first section of bleachers.

"Well, shit. Mission accomplished."

That voice was immediately recognizable. Pierce. He sounded out of breath, like he'd just gotten off the ice. So he was here early to practice, not because he cared about the workshop. Oh well. At least he was here on time today. I pressed my back up against the door, ready to make a quick escape if needed, but I wanted to hear this conversation. I wanted to hear if Pierce one-on-one with someone else was more like online Pierce.

"Dude, I told you. You're going to be fine. Coach isn't pissed, he's going to work through this with you, and you're going to turn it around."

Coach. The capital-C form. So it had to be another player from the NTDP team, slumming it at the Troy rink. Maybe there wasn't any ice time available at the team's Plymouth rink. If there was one thing Mr. Kozlov had an excess of, it was ice time.

"Whatever you say," Pierce muttered.

"Damn right, whatever I say." There was the plastic click of a water bottle hitting the inside of a trashcan. "And in the meantime, stay off the forums. They can't get under your skin if you're not looking at what they're saying."

"Slight problem with that, though."

"What?" the other NTDP player asked.

"There's this girl."

The guy laughed. "If I had a dollar for every time you said those words, I wouldn't need to make it into the NHL. I could retire tomorrow."

"It's not like that," Pierce said. "This is different. I don't even know who she is."

My hand clenched around the door handle even as I leaned a little closer toward the conversation. I had to hear this. But all I heard at first was laughter.

"Dude, someone you don't know on an online forum? 'She' is totally a forty-year-old guy. No doubt."

"I know catfishing is a thing that happens, but I don't feel like this is that. She said something that makes me think she goes to Troy Prep."

Crap. I wracked my brain. What in the world had I said that had given away that I went to Troy Prep? I had to be more careful.

"Okay, so maybe the age is right, but how do you know it's not a dude?"

"I just know. But get this. She knows a lot about hockey. Like, professional level stuff."

"So she—assuming she is a she—is a hockey chick? I've never known you to be interested in hockey chicks. And there have been plenty to choose from."

Pierce sighed. "I don't think she's a hockey chick. Not really. She's just…smart. And observant. And knows her shit. But anyway, she's the reason I can't stay off the forums. I haven't asked for her email or to text her or anything, so private messages there are the only way we're communicating."

There was the sound of bags being flung over shoulders and footsteps approaching. I scrambled to open the door and pretend like I'd just walked through it, letting it slam loudly behind me. Pierce and the other player looked over, their conversation coming to an end.

"Oh, hey Lia," Pierce said.

He got my name right! All three letters. It felt like a victory. But the bigger thrill was that Superfan01 was having an impact on Pierce,

"Hi, Pierce."

"Luke, this is Lia. We teach that workshop together. Lia, this is Luke. We play together for NTDP."

"Nice to meet you," I said. Luke offered a handshake. His hand dwarfed mine. He had a few inches on Pierce, and Pierce was tall. As I looked back and forth between the two, I realized Pierce was definitely the better-looking one. Had his hair always had that little curl at the ends? Since when did he have those cheekbones? Did his lips always look like he was on the brink of a smile? Oh God, when did I start thinking about Pierce Miller's lips?

"What?" I asked, when I realized one of them had asked a question and I hadn't been paying attention. My cheeks burned.

"What level figure skater are you?" Luke asked. Then he quickly clarified, "My sister's a figure skater. That's the only reason I know anything about it."

"Junior," I said quickly, hoping to make up for my first delayed response. "But my coach is trying to convince me to go for senior level. I have to pass the test first." I wasn't sure why I was babbling to two guys who couldn't care less about figure skating, but I couldn't seem to stop myself. "Once I pass, I can try for U.S. Nationals and the Olympics."

"Wow, so we're in the presence of a future Olympic gold medalist?" Luke asked.

"No. Maybe. I don't know. I haven't decided if I'm even going to try it or not." Wow, I really needed to just *shut up*.

"You should," Pierce said.

I should. Pierce said so. And as much as I didn't want that to matter, it did.

Before I could respond, the rink door opened again. I thought it might be a workshop kid arriving early, but it wasn't. It was a news reporter from one of the local stations along with a cameraman.

Instantly, Pierce's attention was off me and onto the reporter. "Barbara! Good to see you again!"

Barbara, who was wearing too much makeup and not enough clothing for an ice arena, walked over and air kissed Pierce's cheeks like they were in France. "Pierce, darling. It's wonderful to see you, too!" She pinched his cheek, and I was just grateful it was the cheek on his face. "How have you been?"

"I've been pretty good, thanks. I'm pumped you're covering this story."

Barbara waved him off. "Local athlete and internet star supports his hometown ice arena by helping kids? The story sells itself."

Frustration boiled in my veins. Pierce wasn't doing this workshop out of the goodness of his heart or for the kids or to help Mr. Kozlov and The Ice House. He was doing this as a publicity stunt. Of course. I didn't know why I hadn't seen that coming.

"Barbara, this is my buddy Luke who plays on NTDP with me, and this is Lia." He almost sounded like he was going to try to say my last name, but then realized he didn't know it. "She teaches the workshop with me."

She teaches with *me*? I wanted to point out the truth of exactly what had and hadn't happened during the first workshop session, but I resisted the urge. The cameraman was already setting up his equipment, and I didn't want me blowing up in Pierce's and Barbara's faces to become the next internet meme.

"It's nice to meet both of you," Barbara said, barely glancing at us before turning her attention back to Pierce. "So, I thought we'd do a little Q and A before the workshop starts, and then film a little of you interacting with the kids." She riffled in her bag and pulled out a stack of papers. "I have release forms for the parents to sign." As an aside, she said,

"Wow, it's cold in here. I really should have worn something warmer."

She came to a place called The Ice House and wore short sleeves. What did she expect?

"Oh, here," Pierce said. He removed his sweatshirt and handed it over to her. "I know you won't want to wear it during filming, but it will keep you warm in between takes."

I wanted to puke.

Barbara immediately put it on. "Aren't you the sweetest thing! Thank you. Maybe I'll leave it on during filming. Show my USA Hockey support."

"Hey, I gotta run, but you guys have fun," Luke said, adjusting his hockey bag on his shoulder.

"See you tomorrow, man," Pierce said. "Good practice."

As Luke walked by me, he rolled his eyes a little and said, "Good luck."

I thanked him.

I was going to need it.

Chapter Ten

PIERCE

I collapsed on the closest bench the second the last child was gone. I was more exhausted than I would have been if I'd just played every minute of a double header. With overtime. All of the kids from last week had returned, plus Mr. Kozlov had somehow found a few more to add. Olivia was adorable and I was fine with her attaching herself to me, but the rest of the kids were exhausting. There were just so many of them, and they constantly needed something. Plus, with the camera crew there, I had to be on my game the whole time. There was always the possibility that someone with money would see that news story and want to donate to Mr. Kozlov and The Ice House, or would start bringing their kids there to skate. Now that the crew was gone, I didn't want to be on my game for a good long time. Thank goodness I had a rare Saturday off with no practice or a game that night. Food and some shut-eye were my new plans.

Lia sat on a bench opposite me and started untying her

skates. They were dented and scuffed. Maybe figure skaters were tougher than I thought they were.

"Thank you for your help out there," I said.

I expected a "you're welcome" or maybe thanks in return, but what I got instead was a glance that almost looked like a scowl and a "yeah."

She was probably just as exhausted as I was. I couldn't blame her, so I tried again. "Some of those kids are already getting good. Can you imagine what they'll be like in a few weeks?"

"Even better." The "duh" was implied by her tone.

As I glanced up at her again, I realized she wasn't one of those girls who was going to fall all over me just because of who I was or what I looked like. It had been a while since I had to work for someone's friendship. It threw me off. "What don't you like about me?"

She looked up, her guard dropping a little, as if she were surprised I'd noticed she didn't like me. But her wall went back up almost immediately. "I don't not like you. I don't even know you."

I used a towel from my bag to dry the blade of my left skate. "Okay, I'm not trying to be an ass, but everyone knows me. I'm loud and all over the place, both in real life and on the internet. Being the center of attention is one of my skills. You know me more than you're willing to admit."

She stared into her skate bag as if it held all of the answers. "I don't know the real you. The one who disappears the moment there's a camera crew or group of fans following you."

I winced. As much as I didn't want that to be true, it was. When I thought about it, there were really only a few people who saw the private side of me. My parents. My brother. Sometimes my teammates. The only other time I was completely real was on the forums with Superfan01. So she had a point. She only knew part of me. But clearly she still didn't like what she saw. "Okay, so what don't you like about what you *do* know about me?"

She zipped her bag shut and sat up. She had the perfect posture that only ballerinas and figure skaters had. "You treat everyone who doesn't worship you like they're invisible. It took you four years to learn my name even though we go to the same school and skate at the same ice arena. You act like you're God's gift to high school, the internet, and hockey. Last week, during the first workshop, you came late, played on your phone the whole time, and left early, leaving me to deal with all those kids. The first time we ever really interacted outside of school, you signed my water bottle when all I wanted was something to drink during my skating practice."

At that, I had to laugh. "I'm sorry, *what* about a water bottle?"

She expanded the story, telling me how she got caught up in a crowd and I seemed to just assume that she was there for me instead of for herself. I was torn between being mortified and cracking up. It sounded like something I would do. Something embarrassing, but still. "Lia, I am so sorry about your water bottle. And about your name and the workshop and everything else. Want me to buy you a new, unsigned water bottle? Or should I just write *your* name on it instead to prove that I actually know it now?"

In a huff, she stood and threw her bag over her shoulder. "Can you be serious about anything for five seconds?"

Crap. I stood and followed her, my own bag in hand. "I am being serious! I want to make it up to you."

She turned to me when she reached the door that led to the rest of the ice arena. "Make it up to me by showing up again next week. By being…" Whatever she was going to say disappeared from her lips. "Never mind. Goodbye, Pierce." Then she walked away, letting the door slam in my face.

I sighed and ran a hand through my hair. Girls were so confusing. Especially this one. What did she mean? What did she want me to be? I pushed through the door and walked into the warmth of the ice arena's lobby. Lia was already gone. The smell of burnt popcorn lingered heavily in the air.

Instead of heading to the front door, I went into the pro shop, where Mr. Kozlov was unloading a box of hockey equipment.

"Hello, Pierce," he said as he ripped open some packing tape with a loud *snap*. "How was the workshop? How were the news people?"

I pushed thoughts of Lia out of my mind. "Workshop was good. Less falling than last week, so I think we're headed in the right direction."

"Good, good."

"And the news crew was good. I bet it's going to be a really great story. Did they interview you?"

"Yes." He shook his head and laughed. "I am no good at that stuff. The talking. Told them interview you."

I smiled, imagining the bumbling old man in front of a TV camera, rambling passionately about the rink he loved with every cell in his body. I bet they got some good footage. Hopefully it would be enough to help the rink. "I'm sure you did great." I nodded to the box, which Mr. Kozlov was sliding across the floor toward an empty display. "You need any help with that?"

"No, no. You have done so much already. You and The Lia Bailey. Best skaters at my rink."

Was it my imagination or did Mr. Kozlov sound a little choked up? It had been a big, exciting day with the camera crew and all. Maybe it was just too much for the old guy. "Hey, next time I'm in I'm going to have you sharpen my skates. In a pinch, I had the guy at the Plymouth rink do it. He totally ruined them. From now on you're the only one who gets to touch my skates."

Mr. Kozlov stood from where he'd been kneeling by the display, various joints popping and cracking loud enough that I could hear them across the small room. "You want me to fix them now?"

"No, thank you. They'll be okay. But from now on I'm coming straight to you."

"Good, good. It's an art, sharpening skates. Like chiseling stone."

"And you're the best artist around. All right, I'm off to grab lunch. Have a good day, Mr. Kozlov. Watch for that news story tonight."

Mr. Kozlov was still mumbling something about the art of skate sharpening when I walked out. I dug my keys out of my bag and headed through the front doors.

But when I got to the parking lot, Lia was still there.

Chapter Eleven

LIA

I turned the key in the ignition, hoping and praying that the terrible noise I'd heard from the engine the first time I'd tried to start the car was a one-time-only occurrence. But the noise just happened again, possibly louder this time, and came with a ton of warning lights and error messages on my dashboard. I let my head fall against the steering wheel and sighed.

The car was a beat-up but insanely comfortable Chevrolet my dad had driven for years and years. Mom gave it to me when I turned sixteen. It had more problematic days than non-problematic days, but it usually got me from point A to point B. Of course, on this day when I was already frustrated with Pierce, that would be an exception to the rule.

I checked my phone. Mom would be right in the middle of her shift. No way she could come pick me up. I scrolled through my phone contacts for Uncle Drew's name. He was watching Adam while Mom worked, so I knew he wasn't working. Best of all, when he *was* working, he was a mechanic who had kept my car running this long.

"Lia! What's up, my girl?"

"Hey, Uncle Drew. My car won't start."

There was some sound in the background, but I couldn't tell what it was. "No good," he said. "Are you somewhere safe?"

"The ice arena parking lot."

"Good. Is it the battery? Didn't we just replace the battery a couple of months ago?"

The only thing I knew was that Uncle Drew did whatever he needed to do to keep my car on the road. "No clue."

"Do me a favor. Pop the hood. Don't forget about the release. And be careful, it's heavy."

At least he'd taught me how to do that, but that was where my knowledge ended. "Done."

"Good. Now put the phone on speaker and set it somewhere safe near the engine."

I did. "Now what?"

"Go try to start it. Let me hear what's going on." His voice coming through the speaker echoed slightly off the open hood.

I got back in the driver's seat and put the key in the ignition. Same failure. Same terrible noises. I did it once more for good measure, then headed back to the engine.

"Let me guess," Uncle Drew said, "all kinds of error messages on your dashboard?"

"A ton."

"Yeah, that's not the battery."

"Fantastic. Can you come get me and tow it to your place?"

He hesitated. There was that sound in the background again. "Yeah. Yeah, we can come get you."

"Wait, are you busy? Because if you are…"

"Well, it's just that I brought your brother out to Ford's

test track. We're supposed to be here another hour or so. He's having a really great time, and…"

He didn't have to finish. The times when Adam was doing something safe and with a father figure since our dad had died were few and far between. I couldn't rob him of that opportunity.

"It's fine. Stay. Have fun. I'll go ask Mr. Kozlov for some extra ice time, or maybe help him out with a few things. No problem."

"Are you sure?"

"Positive. I'll be here whenever you get back."

"You're a good niece and sister."

"You're a good uncle."

"See you soon."

I hung up and pocketed the phone before releasing the hood stand. I dropped the hood, making sure to keep my fingers out of the way, and when I looked up, Pierce was standing there. This day just kept getting better and better.

"Car trouble?" he asked.

"Yeah." I picked up my skate bag and slung it over my shoulder, ready to head back inside. Ready to be done with this conversation.

"Want a ride home?"

"No. I'm going back inside until my uncle can pick me up." Despite the fact that it was Pierce, it was a nice offer, so I added, "But thank you."

"Come on. I owe you after the whole 'water bottle' incident. Let me give you a ride."

"I'll just skate some more or help Mr. Kozlov or something."

"That's a nice thought, but there's no way you have energy left for that. Those kids were exhausting." He smiled. "Come on. Please let me make this up to you."

Ugh. That smile. Those eyes that looked so green in the

sun. No wonder he got whatever he wanted. I wanted to tell him no. To show I didn't need or want him. But this sincere Pierce was so close to the online PierceMiller that I couldn't resist. "You don't mind?"

"Not at all." He pulled his keys from his pocket and nodded to the car two spaces over from mine. "Let's roll."

We got settled in Pierce's car, which smelled like pine air freshener with just the slightest hint of hockey equipment. At least it was clean, which couldn't be said of most guys' cars. He pulled out of the ice arena parking lot, turning left without asking for directions. "Aren't you going to ask me where we're going?"

"I'm hungry. Are you hungry?"

"No," I said, but my stomach chose that exact second to give a loud growl. Apparently working that hard with kids was enough to work up an appetite. Blood instantly rushed to my cheeks.

He glanced over and grinned. "Something tells me that's not quite true. Let's get lunch. You have to eat anyway, right?"

"Right, but…"

"No 'but.' You're hungry. You need to eat. Let's eat together. More of that 'making it up to you' stuff."

At that moment, I noticed a tiny Detroit Red Wings banner hanging from Pierce's rearview mirror. It was a miniature version of the ones that hung in Joe Louis Arena. One side had a list of all the years the Wings had won the Stanley Cup. The other listed the retired jersey numbers. My dad's was one of them. I wasn't a big believer in signs, but if I were, I imagined this would be one of them. I sighed, resigned. "Fine."

"Perfect."

But wait…was it perfect? I was going to lunch with Pierce Miller. This wasn't a date, was it? Was this a date? I wanted to slide my phone out of my pocket and frantically text Embry, but that would be too obvious. I left my phone in my pocket and tried to convince myself this wasn't a date, so there was nothing to be worried about. This was just Pierce. The guy I tended to hate. I didn't have to impress him.

"How about Parkwood Cafe?" he asked.

I had driven by there on my way home from the rink a thousand times but had never stopped. "Never been there."

"Really? I love it. Real cooking. None of the processed junk."

"Sounds good."

He turned into the parking lot, which was surprisingly empty for lunchtime on a Saturday. He pulled into a spot and even held the door for me when we walked into the restaurant, causing me to have the date/not date debate with myself all over again.

"Two, please," he told the bored looking hostess at the stand.

Clearly she didn't keep up with hockey, YouTube, or the local news because she didn't even flinch at Pierce's presence. "This way." She led us to a booth and placed two worn menus and two sets of silverware in front of us without another word.

"So what do you like to eat?" Pierce asked. "I can give you recommendations." Then, as if he was too excited to wait for my response, said, "The Superfood Salad is my favorite. Kale and chicken and blueberries and cashews and a whole bunch of other stuff." He turned the page. "The turkey wrap is good, too. Served on this low-carb tortilla they make by hand. The chicken salad wrap is good, too, but I usually go with turkey."

I flipped through the pages, following his quick recommendations with my eyes. "It all sounds good," I said.

"Right? I swear working with those kids burns more calories than an entire game. That is, when I'm not being a jerk or a slacker and playing on my phone the entire time."

When I looked up from the menu, there was a smirk on his face. Two could play at that game. "For a second, I thought the kids were going to have to sign on to the NTDP forum just to get your attention."

Something unreadable flashed across his face and I panicked. Maybe he was one of those guys who could make fun of himself but couldn't be made fun of by anyone else? He didn't seem like that kind of guy, but maybe…

Thankfully his expression changed to a smile. "They're probably better at technology than they are at skating. Poor Olivia. Did you see how many times she fell today?"

"Yeah. Kid's going to have some bruised knees. But at least she wasn't crying this week, thanks to you."

His smile widened. "See, I wasn't all bad last week."

I couldn't help but smile, either. "I guess not *all* bad, no."

The waitress came over to take our orders. I went with the turkey wrap and a side salad. He went with the Superfood Salad, double chicken, double cashews, oil and vinegar.

"I have to say, I think that's the healthiest I've ever seen a guy order at a restaurant."

He finished taking a sip of water and shrugged. "One of coach's mottos is 'eat like crap, play like crap.' And I hate to say it, but he's kind of right." He balled up his straw wrapper and set it on the table. "So, tell me about the whole figure skating thing. Have you been doing it forever?"

"Pretty close. My dad put a pair of skates on me as soon as I could walk." Internally, I winced, but I tried to hide it. It was a slip. The last thing I wanted to talk about with Pierce was my dad. "But I didn't start taking figure skating lessons until I was five."

"That's when I started playing hockey, too. I saw you skate that day. You're good. Really good." He reached for the containers of creamer and sweetener at the end of the table, which was odd considering he hadn't ordered coffee. "So, when am I going to get to watch you during the Olympics?"

"Um, whatever year you decide to sit and watch me while I watch from my couch."

He wrinkled his forehead. "Come on, you seriously don't see yourself on that podium? You're so close."

It was such a Pierce thing to say. For him, everything was within his reach. He probably didn't understand that wasn't how it was for everyone. "No. It's a lot further than you think."

He started building something out of the coffee condiments he'd collected. "Why?" he asked, without looking up from his mystery project.

I couldn't tell him the real reason. That it was my dad's dream for me, and he wasn't here to help or watch it come true. That I thought if I tried and failed, somehow, from wherever he was, he'd be disappointed. "Not everyone can be that good. Why don't you tell me about hockey?"

He gave a quick smile before turning back to the table and starting to place some of the creamer and sugar carefully in front of me. "I'll let you pretend that's a real answer to the question and change the subject…for now. And I will tell you about hockey. Hockey," he said as he handed me a coffee stirrer, "is the thing I've been best at my whole life. Until this season. Now I'm sucking all over the place, which is fantastic because now is when the NHL scouts are really looking."

"That sucks," I said. And it *did* suck. But really I was more focused on how much *this didn't* suck. How natural it was to be with Pierce. To talk with him when he was being honest. In person.

"Yeah. There's a lot of season left. I just have to turn it around. Soon." He looked up at me, mischievous grin on his face. "Aren't you going to block your goal?"

Confused, I looked back down at the table. It was only then that I realized what he had been working on. He'd built a miniature tabletop hockey rink, coffee creamer containers for the rink walls, sugar packets marking the goals, coffee stirrers for sticks, and his balled up straw wrapper for a puck. I smiled and put my "stick" approximately where the goalie would stand. "Game on."

Pierce started pushing the wrapper from his end of the table to mine. "Miller barrels down the ice, puck in his control. He dodges one defender. Then he spins and avoids another. Did you see that stick handling? Amazing! He approaches the net. He shoots…" He wound up and tapped the wrapper toward my "goal." "…he scores! The crowd goes wild."

I picked up the wrapper from where it had landed on my left thigh. "Lucky shot."

He scoffed. "Nothing lucky about it. That was all skill."

"Whatever." I set the wrapper back in the "rink." "You ready?"

"Show me what you've got."

I started tapping the paper, but he stopped me right away. "No, no. You have to commentate your shot."

"Seriously?"

"Is there anything other than serious when it comes to table hockey?"

I sighed and cleared my throat. "Lia takes—"

"No, no, no. Have you ever heard a hockey player called by his first name? Last name only."

"Fine. Bailey skates down the ice."

He laughed with his head thrown back. Not like he was laughing at me, though. Just like he was having fun. "You really are terrible at this, you know that?"

That was good. The less he thought I knew about hockey, the less idea he'd have that I was the daughter of Steve Ziegler or that I was Superfan01. "Maybe you should do the commentating and let me worry about the kicking your butt."

"Deal."

I started tapping the wrapper and let him do the talking.

"Bailey takes control of the puck. Whoa, did you see that move? She evaded two opponents at once! I think that was a double triple toe axel."

I laughed and glanced up at him. "Not a thing."

"Watch out, there's someone coming up behind Bailey, and fast! She'd better get her head in the game!"

"My head is in the game! She shoots…" But I didn't finish the sentence. Because I didn't score. I missed completely, hitting one of the coffee creamer walls.

"See, the goal's over here," he said, motioning to the sugar packets. "Did I not make that clear? The walls…those aren't what you shoot at."

My cheeks warmed a little at his teasing, but that didn't stop me from laughing. I snatched the wrapper and took it back to my side of the table. "Let me try that again."

We kept playing table hockey until the waitress brought over our food, giving us a look that said we had better clean up all of the creamer and sweeteners before we left. Pierce pushed everything to the side just as the score was about to become five to zero or something ridiculous like that. I'd blocked a shot or two of his, but had failed to get the "puck" beyond him even once.

"Thank you," I said when the waitress set a plate in front of me.

"Hey, wait. Didn't you order a salad, not fries?"

There were definitely fries on my plate and no salad in sight. "I think so, but that's okay. This wrap is so huge, there's no way I'll be able to eat a salad, too."

"Sorry, hon," the waitress said. "You sure? They must not have seen the note, but I can get a salad for you."

"No, this is perfect. But thank you."

"So," Pierce said as he drizzled a decent amount of oil and vinegar over his salad, one bottle in each hand, "who do you hang out with at school?"

"Embry Thomas, mostly." Just saying Embry's name made me a little nervous. I couldn't hide this from Embry, but how was I going to explain it? The girl was going to freak. "We've been friends since kindergarten."

"Embry Thomas," he repeated, tapping his fork against his plate and looking up at the ceiling like he was going to find Embry's yearbook picture there. Maybe he did, because he said, "The singer?"

Whoa. Pierce knew who Embry was? And that she was a singer? Girl was *definitely* going to flip. "The really good singer. She just got a solo in one of the songs for their next performance. They're covering songs from *Hamilton*."

"What's *Hamilton*?"

Of course the athlete didn't know anything about musical theater. So stereotypical. "It's a musical. Embry's favorite. She's pumped."

"Does she skate, too?"

I laughed. "She's tried, but no. Her talents are limited to music."

Pierce didn't say anything, but when I looked up, he was smiling. He had just the slightest dimple in his left cheek.

"What?" I asked.

He shook his head and stabbed a piece of kale. "Nothing. It's just your laugh. I love it. So genuine and contagious."

I fought to hold back the awkward giggle that would be anything other than genuine or contagious. I looked down at my plate to hide my warming cheeks. "Thanks. This wrap looks amazing. Good restaurant choice."

We both started eating, continuing to talk mostly about school and hockey in between bites. Soon, my wrap was gone and Pierce's plate was completely empty.

"That was good," he said, "but those fries look amazing."

I picked up a small one and popped it in my mouth. "They're kind of cold by now."

"But still good, right?"

They were. Still crispy on the outside, soft on the inside, and perfectly seasoned. I nodded to his empty double chicken, double cashew plate. "You can't possibly be hungry after all of that, can you?"

"I'm a seventeen-year-old guy who plays competitive hockey and eats healthy. I'm *always* hungry."

I nudged my plate over toward him. "One won't hurt you."

He hardened his jaw and did not look at the plate. "You are a bad influence."

I gave him the laugh he loved. "Come on. Betcha can't eat just one." Now it was a challenge.

"If I play like crap at tomorrow's practice, I'm telling Coach it's your fault."

"Fair enough."

After one last second of hesitation, he reached out and snatched a fry from the plate. As he ate it, he closed his eyes and smiled in this completely adorable way. "I forgot how good French fries are." When he opened his eyes, he flagged down our waitress and asked for a fresh plate of fries.

"Hey." I laughed. "I only told you to eat one, not an entire order."

"Impossible. And I'm not going to eat the entire order. You're going to help me."

"I am, am I?"

He nudged the plate of cold fries aside and started shaking up the bottle of ketchup in preparation. "You are. Hey, why haven't we ever hung out before? Water bottle incident aside, of course."

I considered. I wanted to blame it on him. To say that he was too cocky and too obsessed with himself and his friends to notice anyone else. But deep down I knew that was only part of the problem. The other part was me. I wasn't confident.

I wasn't outgoing. I didn't think anyone like Pierce would want anything to do with me. "I don't know. I guess we just haven't had the chance."

Thankfully before Pierce could say anything else, our waitress appeared with a steaming plate of fries. "Enjoy," she said.

He rubbed his hands together in anticipation. "Oh, we will."

These fries were even better than the first batch. I did eat a few, but Pierce inhaled most of them.

"Okay, you can't possibly be hungry anymore," I said once the plate was empty.

He leaned back in the booth and placed both hands flat on his stomach, as if testing my theory. Then he shrugged. "I could still eat."

I laughed. "We should probably get out of here before you see someone eating pie."

"You're probably right." He picked up the bill the waitress had left.

I tried to give him some cash, but he waved it off. Sharing food? Him paying? If this thing wasn't in complete date territory, it was getting pretty close.

"Thank you."

"You're welcome. Like I said, I owed you. And I had a really good time. I've been so stressed out lately. This is the most relaxed I've been"—he gave me a look I couldn't read—"in a while."

"Good. I had a good time, too."

After paying, Pierce pocketed his wallet and raised his eyebrows. "Ready? I promise to actually take you home this time."

I checked my phone. It had to have been an hour since I called Uncle Drew. Sure enough, there was a text from him saying he'd be at the rink about fifteen minutes from now.

"Actually, can you take me back to the rink? My uncle's a mechanic. He's going to meet me there."

"Can do." He held the restaurant door for me and even opened the car door for me.

What was happening? Was it possible that the Pierce I'd gotten to know and like on the forum actually liked me in real life?

"I had a really good time with you. We should hang out more, outside of school or the workshop."

Oh God. These were things boys said on dates. This was a date. "Okay," I said. Then, worried I didn't sound enthusiastic enough, I added, "I'd like that."

We were back at the rink, and he pulled up right next to my car. Before putting his car in park, he turned to me and smiled. "Good."

Yeah, how had I never noticed that dimple before? How had I never noticed how sweet he could be? Oh God. He was facing me. Was he going to kiss me? Was I going to let him?

He leaned in a little closer. "You don't have a boyfriend, do you?"

I frantically shook my head. Probably a little *too* frantically. "No. Not at all."

"Good." He reached up and tucked a strand of hair that had fallen from my bun behind my ear. "Because I wouldn't want there to be any reason I couldn't do this."

He leaned in, I closed my eyes, and he kissed me, soft and sweet at first. Testing. Exploring. But then I leaned in closer, and soft and sweet was replaced with intensity that stole the air from my lungs, from the car, from the entire world. He cupped one hand around the back of my neck, and the touch tingled every single nerve in my body. He pulled back for just one second, just one breath, and then he kissed me again. Harder. Deeper. His hands slid down my back, and mine grasped at the thin fabric of his shirt—

Until pounding on the window made us both jump.

I looked up to see my brother banging both fists on the window. "Hey!" he shouted, loud enough that I could hear through the glass. "Is this your boyfriend?"

"Who is that?" Pierce asked.

"My brother." A brother I was going to *murder*.

Pierce nodded toward Uncle Drew, who was also approaching the car. "So that makes him your dad?"

"Uncle," I corrected.

"Don't worry," Pierce said quickly. "I got this." He unbuckled his seat belt and got out of the car.

I quickly unbuckled my seat belt and pushed my brother away with the door so I could get out, too. I gave him my most murderous glare as I walked by, but Adam just rolled his eyes.

"You must be Lia's uncle," Pierce said.

"I am. And you are...?" Uncle Drew stood tall and cracked his knuckles, one by one.

"Pierce. Pierce Miller." He extended a hand.

Uncle Drew took it. "Aren't you that USA Hockey player?"

"I am."

I caught Pierce's wince as he said it. "Uncle Drew," I said, "if you break his hand, he won't be able to play hockey."

He let go immediately. "Right. Sorry. I just get a little protective when it comes to my niece."

"Lia and Pierce sitting in a car, K-I-S—" Adam said in a singsong voice.

I turned to glare at him. "Would you shut up?" I hissed. God, for someone who acted like he was fifteen going on twenty-one most of the time, he could still act fifteen going on five. Before I turned back around, I added, "That doesn't even rhyme."

Adam just shrugged. He was no doubt enjoying his moment as the good child with me getting in trouble.

"I understand that, sir. I teach the workshop for Mr. Kozlov with Lia. When I found out her car wasn't working, I didn't want to leave her alone. We went and had lunch. That's all."

I had to give him credit. He worked in the fact that he was volunteering for Mr. Kozlov and called my uncle "sir." He was trying. I just prayed it would work.

Uncle Drew scratched his chin. "Is that so?"

"Yes, sir."

"Did you pay?"

"Of course."

"Good answer." He nodded to me. "But I think we should be going."

Crap. I didn't want to leave. That kiss had been amazing, but it hadn't been enough. As alarmed as I was to realize how much I'd wanted that kiss, I was even more surprised by how much I wanted more. Despite the fact that it might have been a terrible idea, I *needed* more. I didn't know what was going to happen next. I didn't have Pierce's phone number. I didn't know when I was going to get to see him again. I wasn't Cinderella and there was no glass ice skate for me to leave behind. "But what about my car?"

"I'll bring one of the guys with me to get it later," Uncle Drew said. "For now, let's go."

"It was nice meeting you," Pierce said.

Uncle Drew nodded but didn't return the sentiment. Instead, he turned and said, "Let's go, Lia."

Before I could follow, Pierce circled two fingers around my wrist, stopping me.

"Sorry," I whispered, feeling embarrassed and guilty and more than a little angry.

But he just smiled. "Totally worth it," he whispered. Then he let me go.

Chapter Twelve

"Okay, Miller. What's gotten into you?"

Usually when Coach asked that question, it meant I was off my game, but I had been off my game for long enough the question had a completely different meaning. "Having a good day, I guess." It was an understatement. I'd been working on penalty shots, just me and our starting goalie, like we had since the disastrous loss to Bloomington Thunder. The difference today was that I was actually making the shots. Every single one. It was the French fries. Had to be.

Coach scratched at his head under the red, white, and blue USA Hockey hat he always wore during practices. "Jackson," he called to the goalie, "you going easy on him?"

"No, sir." Jackson's voice was muffled through his facemask.

"Good," Coach said, but he sounded hesitant. "Let's do a few more."

I grabbed a puck with my stick and headed back to center

ice. I was trying hard to do what Superfan01 had pointed out—to read the goalie. Granted, reading someone on my own team during a practice was a lot different from reading an opponent during a shootout, but still. I watched for every movement. Every weight shift. Every glance. I used those to my advantage, and the puck went in the net again. And again. And again.

"All right," Coach called after the fifth or sixth shot. "Bring it in."

I skated over to Coach, getting there a second before Jackson. We'd both removed our helmets and were both breathing a little hard.

"What, is it catching?" Coach asked.

Not having any clue what he meant, I asked, "Sir?"

"First you can't get a puck in the net, then you," he nodded to Jackson, "can't keep one out. When you're both having a good day, it's closer to fifty-fifty. What happened to that?"

I thought about what Superfan01 had said. It wasn't fifty-fifty, and I'd just proved that.

"I was trying," Jackson said. "I swear." He turned to me and smiled. "Looks like you're back, man."

I smiled back and pounded the pad on his shoulder. "Damn straight."

"Yeah, yeah," Coach said. "Just make sure this lasts through Tuesday's game, okay? And don't look so happy. You're heading next door to join the rest of the team, and I think they just started wind sprints."

We both groaned, but mine was more for show than anything. I felt good. I just had to keep it going through the rest of the season.

No pressure.

I drummed my thumb against the edge of my laptop. I was supposed to be working on the math homework I'd left until Sunday, but instead I was on the NTDP forums, reading over my private messages with Superfan01. It wasn't that I really wanted to continue failing my classes, it was just that I had other, more interesting things on my mind. I suspected Superfan01's real identity was Lia Bailey. I had spent the last twenty minutes or so searching for clues to confirm I was right. So far I already had a few clues:

1. Superfan01 and Lia both appeared in my life at approximately the same time.

2. When I'd asked the silly question about streaking through school, Superfan01 had said *our* school. Not *her* school. *Ours*. The one we shared. So she had to go to Troy Prep.

3. At lunch, Lia had mentioned the NTDP forums. Which meant there was a chance she had been on them, too.

4. Intuition. Maybe it was the way Lia spoke and the way Superfan01 typed. How similar they seemed. Hell, maybe after lunch had gone so well it was just wishful thinking.

Whatever the case, I needed confirmation before I could confront her about it. Or confront either "her" about it. I didn't want to seem completely crazy if I was wrong. I'd just have to say the right things and ask the right questions to get a confirmation either way.

I started typing a new PM to Superfan01.

PierceMiller: *I did what you said. Paid more attention to clues from the goalie. Made 100% of the shots I took today.*

There was a knock on my bedroom door while I waited for a response. "Yeah."

Dad poked his head in. "How's it going?"

I motioned to my abandoned math homework. "Tell me,

why do I need to learn all of this when a calculator can just do it for me?"

Dad scratched the top of his head. There was a lot less hair there than there had been a few years ago. "Well, when I was a kid, my math teachers used to say we had to learn it because we wouldn't always have a calculator in our pocket. But now all of you literally have a calculator in your pocket all the time. So that's a valid question."

"Exactly."

"Can't you ask me when you're ever going to need to use this instead? I like that question better."

My phone vibrated. Probably a new message from Superfan01. I smiled but tried to play it off. "You're an accountant. I'm not falling into that trap."

"I suppose that's fair. Need any help?"

I assumed Dad didn't mean to ask if I needed help determining if the girl I went out with was also the girl I'd been having long conversations with on the NTDP forums, so I shook my head. "No. But thank you. I'll yell if I get stuck."

"Okay. But don't yell too loud. Carson just went to bed."

"You accountants, always so literal."

"Yeah, yeah. I'll be in my office if you need anything."

I thanked my dad and waited until the door was closed before clicking back to the NTDP site.

Superfan01: *Good! Too bad it wasn't a game day.*

That didn't mean anything. The schedule was online and all over NTDP's social media accounts. Literally anyone could find out it wasn't a game day.

PierceMiller: *Too bad. Do you know what else I think helped? French fries. I ate them yesterday for the first time in a while, and they must have made a difference. Considering making them one of my main food groups.*

Superfan01: *Or maybe it wasn't so much the food, but the fact that you let yourself relax. Maybe when you relaxed your diet, your mind relaxed as well, and enough of the stress you've been under went away so you could focus on reading the goalie and shooting the puck.*

PierceMiller: *How'd you know I've been under stress?*

Superfan01: *You're one of the leading new draft picks for the NHL. Or at least you were until recently... Of course you're stressed.*

Another message came through almost immediately, before I could think of a response.

Superfan01: *Sorry. Just stating the facts. They don't know about your French-fry-powered practice yet.*

Though it stung to be reminded of the fact, I couldn't deny it. The stats were public knowledge, too.

PierceMiller: *It's okay. You're right. They don't know. If they did, I'd be back on top. Absolutely.*

We continued talking, about favorite foods and favorite hockey movies and favorite movie snacks. I was relaxed. As relaxed as I had been sitting across the table from Lia. If Superfan01 was Lia, I didn't know why she didn't just tell me. It wasn't a big deal. Especially now. Now that I'd kissed her. Now that I not only knew who she was, but was seriously looking forward to seeing her at school again.

By the time my dad went to bed and I'd given up on math

homework once and for all, I'd also given up on linking Lia and Superfan01 tonight. I'd try again in person. When she couldn't hide behind a computer and an anonymous screen name.

I was so sure I was right. I *wanted* to be right. If she could make me fall for her twice in two different ways, that was saying something. But what if I was wrong? Not that the thing with Lia was serious yet or the thing with Superfan01 was more than an online connection, but both could be. The thought excited me, but also worried me.

What was I getting myself into?

Chapter Thirteen

LIA

"It was one kiss, Mom," I said, exasperated. "We were in the ice arena parking lot in the middle of the day. It wasn't like anything was going to happen." Mom ended up working a sixteen-hour shift on Saturday thanks to someone calling in sick, so Uncle Drew had just filled her in this morning. Now she was reaming me out at our kitchen counter.

"Yes, and thank you for that, but the fact is that you were out with a boy without telling anyone. You rode in the car with someone we've never met—"

"Because my car was dead!"

"What if he was a terrible driver? What if he'd gotten in an accident?"

"Then you would have taken good care of me at the hospital."

Mom took a sip of her coffee and narrowed her eyebrows at me. "Not funny. Look, I'm not thrilled about this, okay? Pierce Miller is…he's in the public eye. He's had to grow up a lot faster than most kids your age."

"I'm not a kid anymore, either." I tossed my phone from one hand to the other, waiting for a message notification from the NTDP forum.

Mom sighed. "You're right. You're not. But you have to tell someone if you're going somewhere with someone I don't know. Tell me, tell Uncle Drew, tell someone. And no being alone with him somewhere that isn't public, okay? He's a boy. He has hormones. He has…needs."

I almost gagged to hear Mom talking about "needs." "Okay, fine, but can we please be done with this conversation?" My phone chimed and I jumped.

"What's that?" Mom asked.

"Nothing," I said quickly.

"Is it Pierce? If it's nothing, let me see."

I almost groaned. Mom had a "hand over the cell phone, no questions asked" rule that would result in confiscation if broken. But Mom couldn't see that I was talking to Pierce online. That would open a whole new can of worms. I had to change the subject…

"Kat wants me to skate at the senior level," I blurted out.

Mom paused, hand halfway out to grab my phone. "What?"

I'd been meaning to talk to her about this but kept putting it off, mostly because I was terrified and didn't want to think about it, but also because Pierce was a fantastic distraction. But if there was one thing that could get her mind off the boy conversation, this was it.

"She told me to talk to you about it. She thinks I'm ready. Wants me to take a test on the eighteenth in Ohio so I can change my registration for regionals to senior level."

Mom let her hand drop. Mission accomplished. "Wow. Honey, that's huge. How do you feel about that?"

I shrugged. While this was a fantastic conversation

changer, that didn't mean I actually *wanted* to talk about it. "I don't know. Nervous, I guess."

"What part are you nervous about?"

"That I won't pass the test."

"If you don't pass the test, then you just compete at the junior level like you already planned. That's no big deal."

She was right. The big deal was the part I didn't want to talk about. The fact that if I didn't pass, I wouldn't be able to do the one thing Dad wanted me to do. Maybe if he'd lived long enough, his Olympic dream for me would have transformed to something else. College or a career or something more achievable. Or maybe it wouldn't have changed, but he would have been there at my side, cheering me on the whole way.

But now I'd never know. The thought made a lump form in my throat. I tried to avoid crying in front of Mom as much as possible. It was hard enough that her husband died and she had a son who really needed a dad. The last thing she needed was to worry about an emotional basket case of a daughter. I cleared my throat and looked away in case she could see the layer of tears that was now coating my eyes.

"I guess. No big deal."

"You'll be ready by then? Kat will have a new program for you?"

"Same program, we're just replacing a couple of jumps and adding to it."

Mom got up from the counter and checked the calendar on the fridge. "I don't work on the eighteenth. I'll be able to take you. I'll make sure Uncle Drew can watch Adam. Want me to register you?"

I glanced at my phone, where the message notification from Pierce was waiting. What would have happened if I'd said no to lunch with him because I was too afraid? I would have missed out on one of the best days I'd had in a long time. Maybe this test could be like that, too. Maybe once it was over, I'd be glad I did it.

"Okay." I looked up in time to see Mom's grin.

"So exciting! I'll go fill out the registration now." She stood, but before leaving the kitchen, she turned and kissed the top of my head.

The gesture made me feel much younger than I really was. "Thank you," I said.

"You're welcome. Your dad would be so proud of you."

The lump and tears threatened to form again until another thought crossed my mind. The test was on a Saturday. In Ohio. Pierce was going to have to teach the workshop himself. Oh, crap. What had I gotten those kids into?

"Okay, spill," Embry said. "What's so important that you needed me to get here twenty minutes before school started when I could have used that twenty minutes for sleep?"

I ignored the guilt trip. It wasn't that I wanted to tell Embry what had happened between me and Pierce, it was just that the longer I waited to tell her, the more of a problem it would be when she found out. And she would find out. Our school wasn't big enough for things like that to go unnoticed.

I looked up and down the hall. I didn't see Pierce—I doubted he ever got to school early—but there were a few others around that I didn't want eavesdropping on our conversation. "Let's go somewhere private."

Embry's eyes widened. "Wait, this is serious?"

I nodded.

"Oh God, is your mom okay?"

"Yes," I said quickly. I remembered the first time I saw Embry after my dad died. She had cried almost as hard as I had.

"Your brother? Uncle Drew?"

"Everyone's fine," I said. I glanced around again. "I just don't want anyone to hear."

"Thank goodness." Then she whispered, "Is it about a guy?"

I nodded, and Embry's expression changed from concerned to excited. She grabbed my hand and started pulling me down the hall.

"Ouch, you're hurting me," I said as my friend nearly ripped my arm out of the socket.

"It's fine, you don't need your arm to skate. Now come on! I'm going to need the full twenty minutes to get all of the details!"

"Where are we going?"

Instead of answering, Embry pulled me into the music room. There were a couple of students around. One was using the piano to tune a guitar. Another was putting together a drum set. This was not as private as I needed it to be. But then Embry pulled me into a small room along the far wall. The door had two large windows so we could see out and everyone else could see in, but the second Embry pulled the door shut, every ounce of noise disappeared. The piano, the guitar, the students' voices, the clanking of the drum set, all gone. It was the kind of quiet that almost seemed loud.

"Completely soundproof," Embry explained. "Now spill."

"How is that possible?" I asked, running my fingers along the seam where the door closed.

"Science," Embry said. "Don't change the subject. I wondered why you were so quiet yesterday. I just wish you would have told me it was because of a guy. Did Brandon call you again?"

Brandon was one of our classmates and the last guy I had dated. Embry had been totally fine with Brandon, up until the day he cheated on me, of course. But Pierce? I had no idea how she was going to react to this news. I had a few theories, but none of them were good.

"No. Not Brandon." I nodded to the wooden piano bench, empty except for a few pieces of sheet music. "Maybe you should sit down for this."

Embry sat and her elbow brushed up against a few of the upper keys, releasing a few high notes.

I checked behind us, through the windows of the soundproof door, just to make *sure* no one had heard that. Then I took a deep breath and said, "Pierce Miller kissed me."

"*What*?!" Embry shouted.

So much for the "sitting" thing. The soundproof room had definitely been a good idea.

"Wait, wait." Embry rubbed at her ears. "I don't think I heard you correctly. I thought you just said Pierce Miller kissed you."

"That is what I said."

Embry collapsed back on to the piano bench and leaned forward. "Tell me everything."

I ran a hand through my hair and tried to convince myself I hadn't skipped my usual bun, instead drying and straightening my hair, because of Pierce. Okay, not *just* because of Pierce. Then I took a deep breath and explained what had happened on Saturday.

"How was the kiss?" Embry demanded the second I finished talking. "It was good, right?"

I couldn't stop the smile that formed on my face. "It was short but sweet. A good first kiss. Or at least it was until my brother started banging on the car window."

Embry winced. "Seriously?"

"Seriously. He and Uncle Drew showed up at the exact wrong second. If he hadn't been a hockey player, I think Uncle Drew might have killed him."

"Ouch. But oh my gosh. I can't believe you kissed Pierce Miller. I can't believe those words just left my lips. You kissed

Pierce Miller."

I set the sheet music on the back of the piano and sat next to her on the bench. "Is that okay? I mean, I know you liked him…"

Embry waved off my concern. "I liked him in the same way I liked the guy in that toothpaste commercial: cute but I'll never have him. I'm just glad you finally came around and realized he's not as bad as you thought he was."

"No, he's not. You were right."

"I'm *always* right," Embry said with a smile and a nudge to my shoulder. "So what now? Are you going out with him again? Wait." She held up one finger. "You are not allowed to eat lunch with him. One date and one kiss do not surpass our years of friendship."

"I'll never abandon you," I promised. "And I don't know what's next. We didn't get to talk after Uncle Drew showed up, and we didn't talk yesterday." But as soon as those words were out of my mouth, I winced, because we *did* talk yesterday.

Of course, Embry could read me right away. "What? What's wrong?"

I hesitated. To confess to what I'd done, the anonymous account and comments, felt embarrassing. But if anyone would keep my secret and help me figure out what to do about it, it was Embry. So I took my phone out of my pocket, tapped over to the NTDP forum, and opened my PMs with Pierce. Then I handed the phone over to her.

As Embry scrolled down, her forehead wrinkled. "Wait, who is this? When did this conversation happen? Is he flirting with some other girl?"

I pointed to myself and said, "Superfan01. He just doesn't know that."

"Wait. What? You're going to have to explain."

I stood and started pacing the short distance from one wall to the other. "I made the account so I could comment on this post where he needed to be called out but no one else was doing it. That was all I meant to say. But then he ended up being so real and genuine…" I shook my head. "I don't know. It's ridiculous, but I enjoy my time with him online as much as I enjoyed my time with him at lunch."

"So…let me get this straight. You're in not one, but two relationships with Pierce Miller."

I hesitated. I didn't know if either one actually qualified as a full-fledged relationship. With one, we'd only gone out once and had one kiss, and with the other he had no clue who I was. "I guess so? Maybe."

"But he doesn't know that."

"Right. And I haven't told anyone that I'm the girl online, so you can't say a word. To anyone."

Embry made a "locking her lips and throwing away the key" motion. "You are going to tell him at some point, right? I mean, that might get awkward if he has to choose between the two of you…"

"Right, but I can't imagine telling him." My cheeks flushed at the thought of confessing what I'd done. "*That's* awkward. Plus…" I bit my lip.

"Plus…" she said with a "please continue" wave of her hand.

"It's pretty clear he's into Superfan01, right? There's absolutely no way he'd be into me."

She frowned and wrinkled her forehead. "First, false. Any guy in their right mind would be into you, including Pierce, who kissed you. Second, how would it even be possible for him to be into Superfan01 and not into you when you *are* Superfan01?"

"I don't know." I groaned and paced back and forth in the tiny room. "I can't explain it, really. I want to tell him. I'm just afraid."

"So you're just going to see what happens?"

"Yeah. I mean, it was one kiss. He might not want to repeat it as much as I do." Just saying the words made me sad, but I also knew I couldn't get my hopes up. I glanced at the lock screen on my phone again. "But for now, the bell's going to ring."

Embry sighed. "You expect me to focus on singing after this? You are a cruel, cruel friend."

I smiled. "Sorry. Can we ignore class and hang out in here and talk all day?"

"Maybe you can," Embry said. "But my class is right outside this door, and I think someone might notice me. Besides, you have a guy to talk to."

"Yeah. Not that we have any classes together. And not that I have any clue what he's going to say."

"Hey." Embry stood and gave me a hug, tugging once on the back of my hair. "No matter what happens with either one of your Pierce Miller relationships, you know I'm here for you, right?"

"Thank you. That means a lot. Thank you for not freaking out or calling me crazy or anything."

"Never."

"Oh, and just so you know? We were talking about friends at lunch, and Pierce definitely knew you as 'the singer.'"

Embry squealed in a way that probably wasn't doing anything for her vocal chords. "Seriously?"

"Seriously. You have a reputation."

"A reputation with the guy who has a reputation," she said, but quickly held up a hand. "Not that you have anything to worry about. He's all yours. I'm just glad to know all my hours of work out there have paid off," she said as she motioned to the music room.

The bell must have rung, not that we could hear it, but there was a definite flurry of activity outside the practice room windows.

"You're both an amazing friend *and* a rock star." I opened the door, and the sound rushed in like a tidal wave. It was amazing how loud a few students and instruments were after complete silence. It was amazing how much background sound I constantly tuned out without realizing it.

"Good luck," Embry said as she squeezed my shoulder.

Only then did the flurry of activity in the music room match the flurry of nerves in my stomach. What if Pierce realized he'd made a huge mistake by kissing me? The possibility of him liking the online version of me than the in-person me was very real. And what if he found out I was lying to him?

As much as I wanted to go back to the quiet comfort of the practice room with my best friend by my side, I took a deep breath, walked into the hall, and went to find out what would happen next.

Chapter Fourteen

"Tomorrow's going to be better," Robbie said as we walked down the hall. "You've got a good practice under your belt. That's all you needed to get your head back in the game."

I quirked an eyebrow at my friend. "Where'd this cheerleader act come from? Should I get you a skirt and some pom-poms?"

Robbie flipped me off and laughed. "Fine. You're going to lose. Terribly. You're going to miss every shot you take and fall flat on your face. Literally *and* figuratively."

Now it was my turn to laugh. "That's more like it." I was about to continue when I saw Lia at her locker, removing some books. "Hey, I'll catch up with you in a few, okay?"

"Okay," Robbie said with a shrug. Then he must have followed my gaze because he asked, "Is that the figure skater?"

"Yeah. Lia."

"Huh. Would not have pegged her as your type."

"She's not," I said. "And I think that might be the best

thing about her." I clapped his shoulder and walked over to Lia, who had her back turned to me. I leaned on the locker next to hers. "Hey."

She startled and almost dropped the book she was removing from her locker. Even though it was loud in the hallway, it was almost like she didn't expect anyone to talk to her. A smile formed on her lips. It was a far cry from the annoyed looks she'd given me at the first workshop. Given the whole "water bottle" incident, those made sense. The look she gave me now was something completely different—sweet, but almost shy.

"Hey," she said back.

"Did your car get fixed?"

"Yeah. My uncle replaced a part, and it's working fine now."

Honestly, I kind of hoped she would still be without a car on Saturday so I could give her a ride. But I'd just have to find another reason to see her. "So do we really not have one single class together this semester? Oh, wait. You're in all of those super smart AP classes, aren't you?"

Her gaze immediately dropped to the floor, like she was ashamed not only of what classes she was in, but of who she was. "I'm not smart. Not really. I've just worked really hard, and—"

"Hey." I used one finger to gently lift her chin. "It's fine. It's good. I just thought that if we're not going to see each other in class, I should probably get your number so I have a way to talk to you before Saturday without having to hope I randomly run into you in the hallway."

"Oh. Yeah. Okay. That would be good."

I pulled my phone from my pocket and created a new contact. I considered putting Superfan01 as the name, seeing how she would react, but I didn't want to take that chance. Not yet. Instead, I put in her name.

"Actually, it's i-a," she said.

I erased the e-a-h I'd typed and put it in correctly. "I like that. It's pretty."

"Thanks. When I was a kid I hated it because I couldn't find it on key chains or pens or anything in souvenir stores. But now I like it."

I handed over my phone so she could type in her number. "I feel your pain. Whatever list of common baby names they use to print those things, Pierce is not on that list. I'm named after some city in Florida that my parents drove through when my mom was six months pregnant."

She handed the phone back. "Creative. I bet your name will be on the common baby names list, though. Once you're a famous player in the NHL, your name will become trendy. All hockey-loving parents will name their sons Pierce, hoping they turn out just like you."

I laughed. "You think so?"

"Absolutely."

"Well, if that's the case, then the superior spelling of Lia will become popular, too. Nine months after you win the Olympics, watch out." Was it my imagination, or did she visibly pale at the word "Olympics"?

"Maybe," she said, but there wasn't any enthusiasm behind the word.

"So, how much trouble were you in on Saturday?"

"A little." She closed the locker. "My mom will get over it."

"Good."

"Hey, Miller," someone yelled, distracting me from the conversation.

When I looked up, it was the quarterback of our school's football team. The team absolutely sucked, but Bronson was a good guy.

"Bronson. Hey."

"Going to pull out a win tomorrow night?" Even though he was past us in the hall, he turned around and walked backward so he could hear the answer.

"Gonna try."

"All right. See ya, man." Bronson gave a wave and continued down the hall.

"Don't do that," Lia said, drawing my attention back to her.

"Don't do what?"

"I just watched every single one of your muscles tense up the second he mentioned the game. Don't set yourself up for failure. Breathe. Relax."

I took a deep breath and felt tension leave my body, tension I hadn't even realized was there. "Thanks. Can you come to the game tomorrow? Sit on the bench with me and tell me to calm the hell down?"

"I have an extra practice tomorrow. Have to get ready for my senior level test."

I was about to ask what that meant when I remembered our conversation from lunch. "Wait, senior level? Like 'first step in trying for the Olympics' test?"

"Exactly like that." She did not sound enthused.

"Don't do that," I said.

"Don't do what?"

I squeezed her shoulder. "I just watched every single one of your muscles tense up the second I mentioned the Olympics. Breathe. Relax."

She smiled and her shoulder did relax under my touch. "Touché. Thanks."

"Welcome." I let go and pushed off the locker I'd been leaning against. "Hey, I meant to ask you, was your uncle a hockey player? He looked so familiar."

Was it my imagination, or did she pale a little? "No," she said quickly. "Not at all. Oh and by the way, my senior level test is on a Saturday, so you're going to have to handle the workshop by yourself, okay?"

By myself? She couldn't be serious. I must have heard her wrong. "Wait, what?"

She closed her locker and headed down the hall, the opposite direction I needed to go. "I checked your schedule. Your game on the eighteenth isn't until later in the day. Thanks!"

Oh, shit. She was serious. I laughed mostly out of disbelief. "I can't handle all of those kids by myself," I called down the quickly emptying hallway. "What will I do with them?"

She just gave a little wave before disappearing around a corner.

I let out a long sigh, then jogged in the direction of my next class. When I got there, I slipped my phone out of my pocket and hid it under my desk. I opened a message to my newest contact.

Me: *You know if I'm in charge of those kids we're going to play ice dodge ball and eat ice cream the entire time, right? None of that "basic skills" stuff.*

Me: *PS - The spelling of your name isn't the only thing that's pretty.*

Then I set my phone aside and tried to pay attention to class, but I couldn't help but think that waiting for a response felt very familiar.

Chapter Fifteen

LIA

I pulled my legs and arms in tight for my final spin, letting the rink blur around me. In the middle of the program, when I still needed my balance, I'd try to spot, but at the end I replaced spotting with every last ounce of speed and energy I had left, not caring how dizzy I got. The music reached its close, and I stepped out of the spin and into my final pose, breathing hard.

Kat clapped from the ice near the penalty box where she'd been watching the whole thing. "Very beautiful, Lia. Very good."

I put my hands on my hips and skated slowly over to Kat, catching my breath. Those extra thirty seconds were taking a lot out of me. "I two-footed the double lutz."

Kat waved me off with a mittened hand. "It was a touch down, not a full two-foot landing. Much smaller deduction."

I picked up my water bottle and took a long swallow instead of responding. The program had been a lot rougher than she was letting on, but arguing with her never went well.

I glanced up at the clock. My practice was about halfway over, and Pierce's game was about thirty minutes in. All of first period was over and part of second. I was dying to know how it was going.

"Let's work on the new footwork sequence and that lutz, okay?"

I nodded and took another drink. "Can I check something on my phone real quick?"

I must have looked completely exhausted, because Kat nodded. Usually I wasn't allowed to even think about looking at my phone during practice.

"Go ahead," Kat said. "Take a breather. I'll get your music queued up to the footwork sequence."

I grabbed my phone and used the touch screen gloves I'd gotten for Christmas to unlock it. I opened the browser and headed over to the NTDP page. There was a scoreboard showing the time remaining in the second period and the current score. NTDP was down by three. That couldn't be good.

Occasionally someone at the game posted updates in the forum, so I headed over there. I wasn't sure which would be worse: to see that Pierce was playing (and was obviously doing rather terribly) or that he'd been benched. But the most recent post was from earlier that afternoon. I clicked refresh just in case, but no such luck. I would just have to worry about Pierce until later.

"What's going on online?" Kat asked.

"Nothing," I said quickly, closing the browser and putting my phone to sleep.

Kat smiled as she put her mittens back on. "I know that 'nothing.' Sounds like a boy kind of 'nothing.'"

I hoped my cheeks were still red enough from the exertion of the long program that she couldn't tell I was blushing. It would just be too weird to talk to my mitten-clad, graying-hair-in-a-bun, earmuff-wearing coach about Pierce. "It's not," I said, a little white lie. After all, I wasn't just looking out for Pierce, I was looking out for the team.

My cheeks must have reached a new level of red, because Kat smiled and said, "Mmhmm. Take one more drink, put that boy out of your brain for now, and let's work on footwork."

By the end of practice, I'd used every last drop of energy I had. We'd worked on footwork and straightened out the kink in the double lutz, but I'd completely forgotten the second half of the program once, and fell on three different jumps the next time.

"I don't think I can do this," I said, taking a sip from my water bottle so I wouldn't start crying.

"Yes, you can. Don't let one shaky practice get under your skin." When I didn't respond other than to take another sip of water—we'd had way more than one shaky practice, so what was I supposed to say?—she sighed. "You'll see. When the test starts, it will be just as natural for you as it was when you passed the junior test."

I forced a nod and tried to believe her.

We both stepped off the ice after putting on our blade guards. "So you're all set, right? Your mom took care of registration?"

"Yeah. All set." The words came out more tense than I intended for them to be.

Kat squeezed my shoulder, where I'd abandoned my sweater about twenty minutes ago, leaving just the thin spandex skating dress. "You're going to be fine. Either way, you're going to be okay. But I think it's going to be great." She picked up her bag. "I have a group lesson next door. I'll see you Thursday?"

I almost groaned. I was pretty sure I was still going to be exhausted and sore by Thursday. But I said, "See you Thursday. Thanks, Kat."

I flopped down on the bench near the rink's entrance, but instead of immediately removing my skates, I removed my phone from my bag. I refreshed the page that was still open to NTDP's site, and then winced. It was now five to nothing with very little time left in the game. When I headed over to the forum, there was exactly one new post. The subject line read *Pierce Miller: Overrated.*

I clicked into the post, which was filled with all kinds of criticism about Pierce's mistakes during this game and recent games. Oh God. Pierce was going to be *crushed.* It was one thing to have a bad game. It was much worse to be called out for it so publicly.

I removed my skates and headed out to my car. I cared more about Pierce's loss and that post than I did about my practice or the upcoming test. So soon and already I was into this thing with Pierce so deep. I wasn't sure if that was good or terrible.

It was nine-thirty when I texted Pierce, well after the end of the game. I decided to play dumb, like I hadn't seen the NTDP site at all. That was probably my safest bet.

Me: *How was the game?*

He didn't respond, so I headed over to the NTDP forum while I waited. There were a few new posts about the game, a few new videos of some of the other team's goals. On the thread about Pierce, several people had commented about the various plays he'd botched and shots he'd missed. No one had stepped up to defend him or say anything he'd done well. Ouch. My phone buzzed and pulled my attention away from the computer screen.

Pierce: *It was okay. We lost. Again.*

Well, "okay" was putting it mildly. But he didn't know that I knew just how bad it was. The phone buzzed again before I could respond.

Pierce: *How was practice?*

So he didn't want to talk about it. Good to know.

Me: *Tiring.*

I wanted him to open up to me, to be honest and real like he was with me online, but it didn't seem like that was going to happen. As far as he knew, I knew nothing about hockey other than what I learned from sharing rinks with various hockey teams over the past ten years. I was too worried about what would happen if I told him that wasn't the case. The last thing I wanted was to get in a conversation about my dad. It didn't matter how many years it had been since he died. It still hurt like it was yesterday.

Then another thought wormed its way into my mind. What if the reason he wasn't opening up to me through text was because he liked Superfan01 better then me? Yes, he'd kissed me, but this was Pierce Miller. That probably meant a lot more to me than it did to him. Maybe the only reason he kissed me was because he *couldn't* kiss Superfan01.

Pierce: *Tiring? Come on. Figure skating can't be nearly as exhausting as hockey, right? ;)*

Even if he hadn't added the emoji, I could imagine the tilt to his head, the twinkle in his eye he got when he was trying to make someone laugh, which really seemed like most of the time. I allowed myself a small smile.

Me: *Oh, definitely not. We actually just take long naps*

in the middle of the ice.

Pierce: Thought so.

While my fingers hovered over the touch screen keyboard, the phone buzzed again, but not with a text this time. With an NTDP message from Pierce. Great. Okay. This was okay. I could do this. I could have two different conversations with the same guy on two different platforms without messing it up.

First, I responded to Pierce's text.

Me: *How was the rest of your day? Besides the game?*

As soon as that was sent, I tapped over to my browser to read the PM on the forum.

PierceMiller: *Well, that sucked.*

My heart broke for him. The bad games and bad playing were stacking up. For a guy who based his whole life, his whole self, on winning and playing well, it had to hurt. And yeah, it hurt me that he was opening up to the online me more than the real one, but I couldn't call him out on that. I'd just have to be there for him in any way I could.

Superfan01: *Sorry. :(You okay?*

Pierce: *It was fine. Looked for you at lunch, but didn't see you.*

That was largely intentional. With half the school crammed into one room, the cafeteria was a mess of chaos and noise. Embry and I tried to stay on the fringes. But I still couldn't help but smile at the fact that he'd been looking for me. Maybe he did like me a tiny bit.

PierceMiller: *Yeah. No. I don't know. Honestly at this point it would be easiest to just quit.*

Even as my heart sank, I knew it would be. Easier to be off the team than to sit the bench. Easier to not play than to play, mess up, and be torn apart for it in the public eye.

Superfan01: *True, but you're not doing this because it's easy, right? You're doing this because you love it?*

When I switched back over to my text messages, I almost forgot what we were talking about. School. Lunch. Right.

Me: *Was sitting with Embry. My turkey sandwich was not nearly as good as Saturday's French fries.*

PierceMiller: *True, but I'm not doing it to lose, either. I do love it. I could do without the public shaming, though.*

Pierce: *Neither was my chicken and vegetables. I have been forever ruined by our lunch together.*

Pierce: *In a good way. :)*

Whoa. Pierce's messages were coming so fast I couldn't keep up with them, let alone reply to them. How was he doing this?

Superfan01: *We'll just have to try to find something to beat the French fries. Loaded tater tots? Hot fudge sundae?*

I was just about to hit "Send" before I realized I'd typed that into the private message instead of my text messages. I hit the delete button as fast as I could. That would have been *bad*. There would have been no way to explain my way out of that one. I re-typed the message in my text messages and hit send, then headed back to the forum to respond appropriately there. In the meantime a text showed up.

Pierce: *Make it a brownie hot fudge sundae and I'm in.*

My fingers hovered over the keyboard. He was making this look way too easy. And he didn't *know* he was talking to the same person in two different ways. Would it be that much harder for him to be talking to a third girl? A fourth? Brownie sundae or no brownie sundae, I was going to have to keep my guard up.

Chapter Sixteen

PIERCE

"That's Pierce Miller!"

When I looked in the direction of the urgent whisper, a young hockey player and his mom were just leaving the rink where I was walking in, hoping to squeeze some extra ice time out of Mr. Kozlov.

"You can say hi," the mom said, smiling at me.

"Hi, Pierce Miller!" the boy said.

As they approached, I could tell that he was maybe a year or two younger than Carson. "Hi, Sean," I said, reading the name embroidered both on his jacket and hockey bag.

Sean's eyes went wide. "How do you know my name?"

I laughed. "I'm just smart like that." The mom stifled a laugh, too. "Did you have a good practice?" I asked.

"Yeah! My team is undefeated!"

Must have been nice. "That's good. Really good. Keep up the good work, okay? Nice to meet you."

"Thank you," the mom said. "We saw you on the news the

other day. Great story."

"Thanks," I said, and nodded to The Ice House. "This place is like home."

"Hey, Pierce Miller?" the boy asked before we parted ways.

"Yeah?"

"Why don't you win anymore?"

Ouch.

"Sean, that's not polite," the mom quickly hissed. To me, she said, "Sorry."

"It's okay. He's not saying anything I don't know. I hope to turn that around soon." I nodded to the building in front of me. "That's why I'm here to practice. In the meantime, you keep winning for me, okay?"

"Okay. Bye, Pierce."

Shaking off the sting of the conversation, I headed into the arena. Mr. Kozlov was at the counter, talking on an old, corded phone that he refused to replace with either a cordless phone or a cell phone.

"Yes, yes. Saturday morning very busy. Sunday afternoon can be possible." He flipped through the paper calendars, which he also refused to replace with more modern scheduling systems. "Sunday afternoon is ready for you."

I leaned against the counter and Mr. Kozlov smiled his crooked smile at me.

"Yes," he said to the person on the phone. "Yes, that is good. See you soon." When he hung up, he started searching for something. "Business is good, Pierce. Phone is ringing. People are skating. Workshop and news story is working."

I smiled. He sounded happier than I'd heard him in a long time. "That's great," I said. I didn't mention that it was a good thing the workshop and news story happened early in my sucky season instead of later. "What are you looking for?"

"Pencil. They grow legs," he said, making a walking

motion with two of his fingers.

"Try behind your ear," I said, laughing along when he retrieved it and laughed at himself.

He penciled something in on the calendar. "What can I do for you? You are not on the schedule tonight, no?"

"Right, I'm not. But I was hoping if you had any open ice, I could squeeze in an extra practice. God knows I need it."

Mr. Kozlov gave me a look, but not one of sympathy like so many people had been giving me lately. One of empathy. It was a world of difference. "You only fail if you give up on you."

I smiled. "True. And that's why I'm here. So, ice time? Is anything open?"

He flipped the calendar back to today. "Rink two. Just don't go in the bleachers."

I quirked an eyebrow. "What happened to the bleachers?"

"Broke. They were as old as me, but…" He smiled. "Good thing no one got hurt."

Poor Mr. Kozlov. Guy couldn't catch a break. "Very good thing. I'll stay on the ice. Thank you." I started to walk away, but then leaned back on the counter again. "Hey, Lia's here, right?"

"The Lia Bailey? Yes, she is here."

"Which rink is she in?"

The smile on Mr. Kozlov's face widened. "You have break on her?"

Certain I hadn't heard him right through his thick accent, I asked, "Sorry, what?"

"You have a break on her?"

I shook my head. "A break? What?"

Mr. Kozlov waved off my confusion. "You know…teenage boy and teenage girl. Kiss, kiss." He made some motions with his hands that I guess were supposed to signify two people kissing.

"A crush?"

"Crush? Not break?"

I laughed. "Right. A crush is what happens when you like someone. A breakup is what happens when you stop liking them."

He smiled. "But you don't break The Lia Bailey. You crush her."

I laughed. He was a crazy old man, but I loved him. "Exactly. So which rink is she in?"

"Rink one."

"Thanks, Mr. Kozlov. See you later."

I headed over to rink one, which was the biggest rink at The Ice House with the biggest sections of bleachers. When I used to play here, it was always the rink I played in. Brought back memories as I opened the door.

But those memories fell away the second I saw Lia. She wasn't on the ice yet. Instead, she was on the ground near a bench and her skate bag, stretching. She was sitting with each leg out to the side, legs perfectly straight, toes perfectly pointed, left arm up over her head and stretching toward her right foot. Whoa.

"Hey," she said, smiling as she sat up.

"Hey."

She nodded to my hockey bag. "Getting in some ice time?"

I dropped the bag and sat on the ground across from her. "Yeah. We have the night off, but…"

"But a night off isn't going to get you back where you want to be."

"Exactly." I motioned to her split position. "Please. Continue."

She smiled and reached her right arm up over her head, stretching toward her left foot.

"How long did it take you to be able to do that?" I asked.

"I guess I learned when I was kid. And once you can do it, as long as you keep it up, you don't lose it." She pulled her legs out of the split position and stretched them out straight in front of her. Her feet almost reached mine. She circled her arms up over her head before bending forward, her nose at her knees and her hands at her toes.

"Okay, how did you do *that*?" I asked. "I can barely reach my knees."

She laughed as she sat up and tipped her chin up at me. "Let's see."

I straightened my legs so they were parallel to hers and stretched as far as I could, which wasn't very far. "See?"

"Your hamstrings are tight. Here, sit up." She stood and walked behind me. "Okay, point your toes a little."

"Only because I'm secure in my masculinity." I could practically hear her eye-roll.

"Right. Now reach your arms up like I did."

I did, fingertips brushing the soft fabric of her sweater. "Okay."

"Now you're going to take a deep breath. When you let it out, bend forward, tucking your chin and reaching as far as you can."

"I feel ridiculous," I admitted.

"Do you want to learn or not? Breathe."

So I took a deep breath in, breathed out, and folded forward. I didn't get much farther than I had the first time. "Not working," I choked out. It was hard to talk around my tucked chin.

Lia laughed and pressed on the small of my back. There were a couple of pops like I was at the chiropractor, which felt amazing, and I felt myself sink an inch or two lower.

"Good," she said. "Now try to relax your hamstrings."

She bent down and stuck her hands under my legs to push on the tight, shaking muscles. When I focused on relaxing those, I got a little farther, too.

"Are you still breathing?" she asked.

I sucked in a breath and laughed when I realized I wasn't. That got me a little farther, too. Not nearly as far as her, but still.

"Good," she said as I sat up. "Do that a couple times a day, and you'll be as flexible as me in no time."

I didn't know about that, but my lower back and my legs did feel pretty good. "What are the odds it will improve my hockey playing?"

She shrugged as she stood over me. "Can't hurt, right?" She sat on the bench and removed her skates from her bag.

I got up, twisting a little and enjoying the looseness in my back, before taking a seat next to her. "Practice in a few minutes?"

Lia tapped her phone's home button to check the time. "Yeah. Kat should be here any minute."

"Not many more practices before your test."

She groaned. "Don't remind me."

I nudged her shoulder. "Don't worry. You're going to be great."

"Thanks, but I'm really not." She sighed and hesitated before saying, "My practices have been terrible lately. It's like I forgot how to land jumps or stay upright and on my feet for four minutes. I just…freeze up."

I frowned. "Sounds like you're psyching yourself out. Why?"

She shrugged. "Don't know."

"What does your coach say?"

"That I'm going to be fine." Lia's phone lit up with a text message. "Speaking of Kat, she's stuck in traffic. Running late."

I got an idea, grinned, and sat next to her, pulling my skates out of my bag. "Perfect."

"Perfect what? What are you doing?"

"I really don't want to go warm up in a rink by myself right now." I finished tying my left skate and pulled on my right. "And your scary coach isn't here to tell me to leave. So until she gets here, let's warm up together."

She didn't move. "Scary coach, huh?"

"Yeah. Did you hear how she talked to me and Robbie? Scary."

"She just doesn't like hockey players. Or people who try to steal my ice time."

I put a double knot in my right skate laces. "That's why we should get started now, before she gets here." I crouched down in front of her and slid a skate onto her foot. It felt a little like Cinderella. "Wait, what the heck are these loop things? How are you supposed to tie these?"

"Here," she said, only laughing at me a little. Then she expertly wrapped the laces around the hooks before tying them in a double knot.

"And I thought the toe pick was the weirdest thing about figure skates."

Lia put on her other skate and tied it. We headed over to the ice, and I let her remove her blade guards and step on before me.

"This is my favorite," she said, pushing a couple of times and gliding almost all the way to the other side of the rink. The magic of freshly smoothed ice.

I followed behind, not having to put forth much effort to cross the ice at all. The only sound was the faint *hush* of our blades cutting into the ice. "It is pretty great," I said. In hockey, it took almost no time for a team to absolutely destroy the surface of the ice. Not that it mattered for us as much as it did for a figure skater. "So how do you usually warm up?"

"Like this."

She started skating down the straightaway, but she wasn't

skating straight. Instead, she was mixing crossovers with just a few steps: *left, cross, left* toward the center of the rink, *right, cross, right* back toward the wall. She repeated this, pushing harder and picking up speed until she hit the turn, then she took all right crossovers until she got to the straightaway again. I followed behind her, mimicking her moves, but not her elegantly held skater's arms.

"That's it?" I asked.

She glanced over her shoulder without missing a beat. "What? Not good enough? How do you warm up?"

The team's warm up usually included drills from Coach. No fun, and right now I wanted to have fun. From what she'd said, she *needed* to have fun. To remember what she liked about being on the ice. So I pushed a little harder, closing the distance between us. "Like this," I said, and then tapped her shoulder. "Tag. You're it." I took off skating in the other direction as fast as I could.

"Hey!"

At first I didn't think she was going to go with it, but then I heard a little laugh and skate strokes closing in on me—fast. I turned before I could hit the boards and pushed off hard, hoping the change in direction would keep Lia from catching up to me as I passed her and headed to the other end of the rink. I laughed as she got close but not close enough, fingers closing around the air at my hip. By the time she regained momentum in my direction, I was long gone.

"Not fair!" she yelled.

"Why not?"

"Because I didn't tag you!"

I laughed. "Try harder this time."

It was actually a good warm up, as far as fun warm ups go. My legs were loosening up, muscles becoming warm, my breathing and heart rate picking up. I weaved back and forth, trying to throw her off, but when I turned to the left and saw that she was already headed my way, I knew I was in trouble.

A smile formed on her face, as if she knew it, too. I skated as hard and fast as I could, but I couldn't gain momentum as fast as she could maintain hers, and soon there were two hands on my hips.

"Got you!"

"Yeah, yeah," I said. "You got lucky."

"Luck had nothing to do with it."

She took off the sweater she was wearing over her skating dress and tossed it on the home team's hockey bench. The dress was a deep green that brought out her eyes perfectly. Like all skating dresses, this one was made of some type of spandex material, clinging tightly to her form, from her wrists up to the high collar and down to the skirt that didn't cover much of anything. It was beautiful. *She* was beautiful.

She skated backward and away from me. "I like this warm up," she said. "Aren't you going to get me?"

I smiled, gave her a second head start, and then took off after her. This time it was my turn to be lucky, making the right turn at the exact time she did, but she pulled some type of ducking figure skater spin move and stayed away from me.

"Hey," I said with a laugh, "no fair! No figure skating moves."

"Why not? It's not my fault that you play the inferior ice-related sport."

Those were fighting words. I pushed harder, my legs protesting the effort, and closed in on Lia. She was fast, but I had several inches on her. When she looked back and saw me approaching, she squealed and tried to head toward one side, but I was too close. She tried to go the other way, but same thing. We were both going pretty fast and the boards were approaching quickly. If she didn't pick a direction soon, it was going to be bad news.

At the very last second, instead of turning one way or the

other, she turned her skate blades hard, coming to a stop just before hitting the boards, facing me, eyes closed, bracing for impact. I threw myself into a stop, too, throwing ice shavings everywhere. Could I have stopped before pinning her to the boards? Yes. Did I? No. I stayed with my skates trapping hers on either side, our bodies touching at knees and hips. Her chest was rising and falling rapidly, breaths warm against my chest, but there was a smile on her face, all traces of worry over her test completely gone. Success.

I kissed one cheek, then the other. I nipped at her earlobe, then tipped her chin up and pressed my lips to the pulse point in her neck. The flutter I felt against my lips was fast, and it only got faster as I kissed my way toward her collarbone. She made this noise somewhere between a whimper and a moan, and I felt it as much as I heard it. Knowing she was that into it was pretty hot. I pulled back and then parted her lips with mine. The last of the distance between us disappeared, and I hoped it would never appear again. Every inch of my mouth tingled. Her hands slid down my skin, leaving trails of goose bumps behind. My brain short-circuited so nothing mattered other than right now.

Reluctantly, I pulled back. We had to breathe sometime. "Got you," I managed.

"You did." She wrapped her arms around the back of my neck and pulled me close. When she kissed me, hard and deep, she made it clear that this time she was the one who got me.

Best warm up ever.

Eventually Lia's coach did show up, so I had to leave and go to my own rink. It was much lonelier without her, but it was a good practice—lots of skating and shooting and puck handling. It was amazing how well I could do when no one else was watching.

I hoped Lia had a good practice, too. She needed it. I wanted to help her, to make her realize that she was an amazing skater who was only freezing up on the ice because she was afraid. If anyone understood that, it was me.

Hmm. If she was Superfan01, I could say something encouraging to her online that might help. Lia could use all the encouragement she could get, from all the places she could get it. If she wasn't Superfan01, the worst I'd do is make someone else feel good. If she was Superfan01, maybe it would be enough to make her spill the truth.

I made sure to finish my practice right around the time Lia would be finishing hers. I wanted to see her again before I left. I packed up my stuff and headed out to the snack bar. Despite the stretching Lia had done with me, my legs were already spent and sore. The sign of a good practice.

"Hey! Miller!" I heard as I took a seat at one of the tables. It wobbled despite a wad of napkins shoved under one of the legs. When I looked up, I saw Justus, one of the guys who played for Troy Prep. I didn't see him much anymore. He was probably in a lot of AP classes with Lia. The kid had always been smarter than the rest of us.

"Hey, man," I said, giving him the three-part handshake we always used on the team. I'd almost forgotten about that. "How's it going?"

"Pretty good." He took the seat across from me and nodded toward one of the rinks. "Here to watch my little sister practice."

"Figure skating?"

He smiled. "Nah. Hockey. She's a total badass."

"That's awesome."

From the corner of my eye, I saw Lia walk out of her rink, bag over her shoulder, water bottle in hand. She said goodbye to her coach and stopped at a table a couple down from mine, digging through her bag. I wondered if she was actually looking for something, or if she was just waiting for me to finish talking to Justus.

"Yeah, she's pretty great." He nudged my NTDP bag with his foot. "So I've been following the team."

I groaned. "Not pretty, right?"

"There's a lot of season left still."

From the corner of my vision, I saw Lia pull out her cell phone and start tapping on the screen. Definitely stalling. Why didn't she just come over and talk to us? After that kiss on the ice, it was easy to forget that she was still shy. "You say that like it's a good thing."

Justus laughed. "It will be good. Things will turn around. I know it. I know you."

"Thanks for the vote of confidence."

"Anytime. Hey, I've been watching the NTDP forums. Who's that Superfan chick? You talk to her like every day."

Crap. I didn't think our conversations were that noticeable. Sure, we commented back and forth a little in the forum, but mostly we stuck with PMs. We'd have to be more careful. Maybe keep it all hidden in PMs. If Coach figured out what was going on, he'd probably try to shut it down. Not that I minded keeping our conversations to myself—

Wait… Was it my imagination, or had Lia stopped typing on her phone and leaned a little closer to hear our conversation? This could be a good test. See how she reacted. So I spoke up to make sure she could hear. "I don't know, man. She hasn't told me who she is, but I think it's someone from our school."

"Really? I haven't read enough of her posts to see that. I just know she knows her hockey shit and seems cool. Who do you think it is?"

I kept my voice loud enough so Lia could hear. "Yeah, she's kind of amazing. I don't know, maybe Ashley Bates? Or

Mara Ramirez?" *There. Let's see how she reacts to that.*

"Your guess is as good as mine," Justus said. "Hey, what about Emma Grady? Doesn't her brother play hockey?"

"I don't know," I said. My view of Lia was blocked for a second as a couple of guys walked out of a rink and toward the front door, laughing loudly. When they passed, I allowed myself a glance at Lia's table, but it was empty. Shit.

"What about her?" Justus asked.

"Who?"

He nodded to the front door, where Lia was walking out. All stalling was apparently gone as she hurried into the parking lot. Crap. My plan had backfired. "Lia?"

"Yeah. Do you know who her dad was?"

"No." Lia had never mentioned her dad before.

"She doesn't tell many people. I only know because we were working on a middle school group project at the time it happened."

"The time what happened? Who's her dad?" Whatever Justus was about to tell me, it felt important. It felt like the confirmation I'd been looking for.

"Her dad was Steve Ziegler."

The rink went quiet as everything fell into place and my stomach dropped to my skates. It made so much sense. Lia knew about hockey because her dad had been the star Red Wings player. She'd probably grown up living and breathing professional hockey, closely watching one of the greats. Learning from him. Maybe even playing with him. Out of all the students at our school, she was the only one who knew enough to make the kinds of comments Superfan01 made. It was the confirmation I'd been looking for. The confirmation I needed. Lia was Superfan01. Superfan01 was Lia. Why wouldn't she just tell me that? It had to be obvious I liked both of them. Liked *her.*

"Hey, where'd you go on me, man?" Justus asked, tapping

my shoulder.

I shook myself back to reality. "What? Sorry. Yeah. Lia. It might be Lia."

Justus smiled. "Man, she is so out of your league."

I laughed the comment off but was kind of afraid he was right. And oh God. Steve Ziegler's daughter had seen me play hockey. Terribly. I'd kissed Steve Ziegler's daughter. He was probably rolling over in his grave.

I was going to be sick.

From across the rink, someone called Justus's name, saving me from throwing up all over my friend. "Hey, I gotta go. Good seeing you, though."

"Yeah, you too." We exchanged the same handshake, but my mind was a million miles away.

Chapter Seventeen

LIA

Amazing. As soon as the word left Pierce's lips, I knew he wasn't going to say my name. And he didn't. He named three or four other girls who knew nothing about hockey, but were more the type to be on his radar. Who he thought were *amazing.* The lack of my name on that list stung more than I thought it would. It was true. He did like Superfan01 better than the real me. I'd suspected it, but now I knew. Setting up the Superfan01 profile had been a mistake. Kissing him had been a mistake. All of this had been a mistake.

I was still angry when I got home, slamming the door behind me. The framed flower print near the door fell off the wall and crashed to the ground. It didn't break, but I swore at it anyway.

"Whoa," Adam said. "Someone's in a bad mood."

It was Mom's day off, and she was sitting on the couch with Adam, some of his schoolwork spread around them. "Hey, hon," Mom said, pushing her reading glasses up on top of her head. It made some of her blond hair stick out in odd directions. "Everything okay?"

"Fine," I grumbled, toeing out of my shoes and leaving them on the rug instead of in the closet where they belonged.

"Rough practice?" Mom asked.

"Practice was fine." My words weren't very convincing, and Mom circled my wrist lightly, stopping me as I tried to walk by.

"Hey, if you two need to talk, I'm happy to excuse myself to my room…" Adam said, starting to close up the book and notebook on his lap.

Mom snapped two fingers and pointed in his direction. "You. Study."

He sighed heavily, his blond bangs blowing up with the motion, but returned to his book. Meanwhile, Mom set her books aside and stood without letting go of my wrist. "Come on. Let's go make some tea."

As much as I wanted to go up to my room and slam my door there, too, I knew it wouldn't make me feel better. Not really. So I begrudgingly plunked myself down on one of the stools at our kitchen counter.

"So, usually your brother's the one slamming doors and swearing and mad at the world." Mom retrieved the teakettle from the cupboard and filled it with water. "What happened?"

I couldn't tell her. I couldn't own up to the fact that I'd created that online account, lying about who I was, even just a lie of omission. That I was using my hockey knowledge from Dad in a way he'd probably never intended. "Nothing happened."

The clicking of the igniter filled the kitchen before the soft *whoosh* of the burner lighting. "Okay, you know I'm not buying that. Did something happen during practice? Did you get hurt? Are you worried about the test next weekend?"

Actually, practice had gone terribly, but I didn't want to

think about or talk about that. "No."

"Well, that's good." Mom removed two mugs from the cupboard. They were delicate china mugs she'd gotten from a garage sale a while back, complete with saucers. Perfect tea-drinking mugs. "So it's something else then. Everything okay with Embry?"

A wave of guilt crashed into me. I'd been neglecting Embry since this whole thing with Pierce started. She'd texted me before practice, and I still hadn't texted her back. "Fine," I said, even though it was less than convincing.

Mom dropped a tea bag into each mug. "Okay, so it's not skating. Not friends. What about school? Something wrong at school?"

That answer was easy. "No."

"Thank God," Mom said. She nodded in the direction of the living room, where Adam was supposedly still working. "I'm having a hard enough time helping with your brother's homework. I can't imagine helping with AP classes."

I didn't say anything, just ran a finger along the edge of the saucer. It was so delicate. So easily broken. I could relate.

"If it's none of those things, then it must be that boy. Pierce."

I still didn't say anything, but my silence must have been answer enough, because she sighed as the teakettle started to whine. She removed it and flicked off the burner before pouring steaming water into each of our mugs. After replacing the kettle on the burner, she took the seat next to me. I didn't know why she was trying. I couldn't open up to her. She couldn't say or do anything to help me. I should have just gone upstairs.

"Spill. What's going on with Pierce?"

I watched as the tea leaves quickly colored the water, changing from clear to light purple to deep mauve. The sweet smell of blackberries wafted up to my nose. "I don't know," I said. "It's complicated."

"Most relationships are."

That was the thing, though. We'd gone out on one date. We'd kissed a couple of times. Did that make us in a relationship? If he still suspected Superfan01 was another one of our classmates, probably not.

"Did he break up with you?" Mom asked.

"No."

"Did you get in an argument?"

"No."

Mom held up one finger and turned her head toward the living room. "Adam! Quit text messaging and get back to work!"

Adam mumbled something about being able to see through walls but presumably went back to work.

"Pierce didn't do anything to hurt you, did he? He didn't try anything…?"

"No," I said quickly. As annoyed with him as I was, I couldn't even imagine that. "Nothing like that."

"Good. Good." Mom cupped her hands around her mug. "I'm afraid I'm out of ideas, then. You haven't been exactly open about this whole 'Pierce' thing, which I get, you're a teenager, but I'd love to be able to help. If I can. Or even just listen."

I picked up my mug and took a tentative sip that still burned my tongue. "I don't know. There are so many other girls who are more Pierce's type than me. I don't think I'm good enough for him."

Mom put her hand on my knee. "Lia. You're smart and beautiful and talented. There are other girls out there, but he noticed you for a reason. Because you're you. Because you're different from all the other girls, in a good way. And if he ever thinks you're not good enough, then *he's* not good enough for *you.*"

"You have to say that. You're my mom."

"Nope. Not part of the Mom Code at all. I just have to make tea. I can say whatever I want. If you were dumb or ugly or boring, I'd tell you."

That made me smile a little. "Gee, thanks."

"Just saying. And hey. I don't know what he said or did today to bring this on, but remember that guys sometimes make poor decisions. Say dumb things. If this was a poor decision, give it a little time. You'll realize that and be able to deal with it. But if it's a bigger issue…if the doubt he causes in you is part of who he is, there will be other guys. Ones who make you feel *more* amazing than you already are."

"Thanks," I said. The only problem was that I had no clue which category Pierce fell into.

"Welcome. Okay. Good talk. I should take my tea and get back to your brother. Five bucks says he's still on the same problem he was on when I left."

I managed a laugh. "No way I'm taking that bet."

Mom pushed the stool in and kissed the top of my head. "See? You're smart. You'll be okay, even if it doesn't feel like it."

I tried to believe her.

The best solution I could come up with was to keep my distance from Pierce, both in person and through textual communication. He sent a private message, and I ignored the notification. He sent a text message asking how my week was going, and I answered with one word: fine.

It helped that it was a travel week for NTDP. The team was playing in Minneapolis, so Pierce was out of school for three days. They lost again and Pierce played terribly again. Not that I was paying careful attention. I just happened to have the NTDP website as one of my bookmarked tabs. I couldn't help but see the score or the summary that went along with it.

Unfortunately, then it was Saturday, which meant avoiding Pierce would be impossible. Hopefully he'd be late for the workshop. We could separate the kids so we didn't have to do any co-teaching, and maybe he'd leave early. But as I was putting on my skates, Pierce walked in. He smiled at me, and my stomach gave a little flip that I hated myself for. I'd been trying to convince myself I didn't miss him, but my body hadn't received the message.

Pierce wasn't alone. Walking next to him was a kid, maybe seven or eight years old, that I didn't recognize from the workshop. Hopefully Mr. Kozlov hadn't added yet another kid to our roster.

"Hey," Pierce said brightly as the two walked over to me. "Long time no see."

He said it like nothing was wrong. But then again, in his mind, there probably *wasn't* anything wrong. He didn't know I was living a dual life. He didn't know that I'd overheard his conversation about who Superfan01 might be, or that it'd have so much impact on me even if I did. The problems here were all mine.

"Who's this?" I asked, nodding to the boy.

"This," Pierce said, playfully resting his elbow on the kid's head, "is my little brother, Carson. Carson, say hi to Lia."

"Hi, Lia," Carson said. "Nice to meet you."

"You, too." At first, I didn't think the two looked that much alike. Carson's hair was poker straight, whereas Pierce's curled at the ends. Pierce was tall and strong, whereas Carson was short and stringy. More importantly, Carson was looking around warily, completely lacking the confidence his brother had in an ice arena. But they shared the same hazel eyes and the same tint of light brown hair.

"Is it okay if he hangs out with us?" Pierce asked. "Our parents had to go to a funeral home visitation."

I could be annoyed with Pierce, but I couldn't be heartless, not when it came to his little brother and not when it came to a death. "Of course. I'm so sorry. Who is it? I mean…was. Was it someone…?" I fumbled for the right question.

He waved off my discomfort. "Someone from my dad's work. No one I knew."

"Oh. Good. I mean, not good. But you know what I mean."

"Yeah," Pierce said, but he was already distracted, bent down and digging something out of his skate bag. He removed a sweatshirt and a blanket. "Arms up," he said, motioning to Carson before tugging the sweatshirt over his head. The static made Carson's hair stand on end.

"How old are you, Carson?" I asked.

"Ten. Pierce, my fingers are cold."

Wow. He seemed a lot younger than that, especially as Pierce pulled first a pair of gloves and then a pair of mittens onto Carson's little hands.

"There," Pierce said. He pulled Carson's hood up over his head and started tying the strings at his chin. "Carson isn't a big fan of skating," Pierce said, glancing up at me, "so I thought he could just sit on one of the benches and watch. Okay with you?"

"Of course," I said.

"Too tight," Carson said, even though the strings were barely even touching his skin.

"Sorry, kiddo," Pierce said, loosening the knot and trying again. To me, he asked, "What did I miss? How was school? How have your practices been?"

It was hard to be mad at him when he was being so incredibly kind and patient with his brother, making sure he was warm and comfortable. "School was same as always.

Practices have been…practices." I bit my lip. "Sorry about another loss."

Pierce shrugged the comment off, but I was getting to know him well enough that I could see it was a facade. He was still upset.

"There," he said, patting the top of Carson's head, where he was now appropriately bundled to spend a couple hours in the ice arena. "Warm *and* handsome. You know, some of the older girls in our group might be almost your age. Maybe we can find you a girlfriend, huh?"

"Ew, no way!" Carson said, like it was the most ridiculous idea anyone in the world had ever had.

I couldn't help but laugh.

Pierce nodded to the bench across the rink. "I'm going to go get him settled. I'll be back to help with sign in."

"Okay. Thanks." As the two walked away, I had to remind myself why I was mad at him. That list of names he mentioned without even thinking about me. Right. But before I could get too upset again, the door opened and Olivia came running in on not-so-wobbly ankles. For a girl who spent most of the first session crying, she seemed like a completely different kid now.

Within a few minutes, the rink was full, and Pierce and I had settled into the routine we'd developed. We split the kids into two ability groups, him taking the more advanced half, me taking the group that still spent more time falling than they did skating, but at least they appeared to be having fun.

"Bend your knees," I told one of the little boys who was still trying to skate completely straight-legged. He did, but bent them so far he collapsed into a giggling heap on the ice. I laughed. "Okay, that was close, but let's try it again." I scooped him up and set him back on his feet.

Over our heads, the scoreboard started buzzing like we were at the end of a hockey game. It was only halfway through our workshop. The clock must have been off.

"That will stop in a second," I said loudly, so the kids could hear me over the buzzer. But it didn't stop as quickly as usual. Maybe the clock wasn't just off, but broken. The buzzer didn't seem to bother the kids, but out of the corner of my eye I saw Pierce skating frantically toward his brother. Turning to look, I saw that Carson had both hands jammed over his ears and was rocking back and forth.

What was happening, some kind of anxiety attack? I wanted to help but didn't want to intrude and make it worse. So I stood motionless while Pierce frantically dug through Carson's bag for something, which ended up being a pair of headphones, a lime green pair of the big, noise-canceling kind that construction workers wore. He jammed them on Carson's head before hurrying over to the controls for the scoreboard, pressing a few buttons before silencing the loud noise.

In the silence afterward, one of the kids yelled, "That was loud!"

The parents who had stuck around to watch the workshop laughed, but I couldn't tear my eyes away from Carson. He was still rocking, clutching at the headphones like they were a lifeline. Pierce tried to pat Carson's shoulder, but he pulled away and kept rocking. Whatever this was, it didn't have an easy fix. I snapped back to attention and motioned for Pierce's group to come join mine.

"Okay, guys," I said. "Sorry about that. Who wants to play a game?"

"Me!" the kids yelled, and Pierce looked over at me gratefully.

I threw together an obstacle course with some hockey cones, a few buckets, and whatever else I could find, and started running the kids through it, helping the littlest ones and the ones with the wobbliest legs. After a couple of minutes, Pierce joined us again, chasing one of the little boys to make him skate faster, which also made him squeal with delight. I looked over at Carson. He was still on the bench, still wearing those headphones, but looking calmer than he had a few minutes before. He was holding Pierce's cell phone, playing a game if the frantic motion of his thumbs were any indication.

"Everything okay?" I asked Pierce when he completed the obstacle course and returned to the start.

He glanced over at his brother. "Yeah. Sorry. Thank you. I'll explain later."

I nodded, and we turned our attention back to the kids. Before I knew it, the workshop was over and the last kid was being picked up. I was exhausted and didn't really have enough energy to deal with Pierce, but he stayed close as we cleaned up.

"Carson has Sensory Processing Disorder," he said, glancing at his brother, probably to make sure his headphones were still on. "Clearly, he doesn't do well with loud sounds. Or certain fabrics. Or certain foods. Or a lot of things, actually."

Oh God. My heart simultaneously sunk to the general vicinity of my kneecap and melted into a puddle at the same time. That YouTube video he'd sent me about mental and developmental health awareness and accepting others. The one I'd judged him for making to appease someone else. That hadn't been some random publicity assignment. That had been Pierce, talking about something way more serious and personal than hockey. He'd been talking about his brother, whom he obviously cared deeply about.

I stacked a couple of cones on top of each other so I could hide the sudden blush on my cheeks. How had I been such a judgmental idiot? "I've never heard of Sensory Processing Disorder. Is that like Autism?"

Pierce put away the two push bars we'd gotten out for the weakest skaters, but they didn't even need them anymore.

More proof that our workshop was successful. "Not exactly, but they do have some similarities." He ran a hand through his hair and looked over at his brother. "I just feel bad for him, you know? Life is so much harder than it needs to be."

I tried to imagine how I would react if Adam had that kind of meltdown. I wasn't sure I'd cope as well as Pierce did. "You're really good with him."

"I just know it's not his fault. Like as much as I desperately want the puck to go in the net, sometimes it doesn't. And as much as Carson wants sounds and smells to be okay, they aren't. I do what I can to help."

It seemed like a very PierceMiller thing to say and do, and I realized that the line between the two Pierces had completely blurred, at least when he was around me. Now I was the only one who wasn't being real. The realization made me feel like a hypocrite.

"Thanks for taking over while I took care of him," Pierce said.

"Of course. No problem."

"I'll let Mr. Kozlov know something's wrong with the buzzer. It did that during one of my practices the other day, too."

"Okay." Another broken thing Mr. Kozlov would have to fix. But as I looked over at Carson, I realized things were easier to fix than people. Than Carson's sensory processing disorder. Than Adam's troubles. Than me freezing up during practices and Pierce freezing up during games. Than my fear of opening up or Pierce's inability to let his true self show, at least at first.

On the bench, Carson looked up from the phone and tentatively loosened the headphones. After a few seconds proved that the buzzer was well and truly done, he removed them completely.

"Is it over?" he asked.

"Yeah, buddy. You ready to go home?"

"Yes," he said with two very affirmative bobs of his head. Then he hopped down, gathered his belongings, and headed over to us. Pierce pocketed the phone Carson had been playing on, and Carson tugged on his shirtsleeve.

"Yeah, Bub?" Pierce asked.

Carson gave me a shy glance, then stood on his tiptoes and cupped his hands around his mouth, presumably so I couldn't hear. "I'm sorry I interrupted your workshop. It was just so loud," he said, loud enough that I could still hear.

Pierce ruffled his brother's long hair. "Don't worry about it. *I'm* sorry we didn't know the scoreboard was broken. I tell you what, how about we play Legos when we get home? That will make our day much better."

"Yes!" Carson started rambling about some ship he was building, and the three of us headed over to the benches at the entrance to the rink so Pierce and I could remove our skates.

"So you're pretty good at Legos?" I asked Carson.

"Not as good as Pierce," Carson said. "But still good."

"He's got a ton of them," Pierce said. "Does your brother like them, too?"

I thought back while I removed my left skate. Adam had Legos a few years ago. Not many, but enough that I remembered cussing him out when I stepped on one that had gotten buried in the carpet. But that was before Dad died, and Adam hadn't done much that was very childlike since then. "Not really. But he might still have some. If he does, I'll bring them for you."

Carson's head whipped in my direction. "Really?"

"Sure. If he's not going to use them, you might as well."

"Pierce, Pierce, did you hear that? Lia's going to bring me Legos!"

"She *might* bring you Legos," Pierce corrected. "And

probably only if you say 'thank you.'"

"Thank you, Lia. Thank you!"

I laughed. "You're welcome." Carson walked ahead of us toward the rink exit, still talking about Legos. Pierce and I followed but hung back a little. "You're a pretty good big brother," I said.

He scoffed. "Pretty good? I think you meant fantastic or amazing."

As much as Pierce's ego tended to get out of control, this was true. I had a challenging younger brother, but nowhere near as challenging as Carson, and I didn't do nearly as good of a job as he did. "Fine. I'll admit it. You are a fantastic and amazing big brother."

He smiled wide enough that his dimples made an appearance, and I forgot why I'd been mad at him in the first place.

"Are you back at school this week?" I asked.

"No. Two games in Canada."

"Oh." I tried to hide my disappointment but wasn't sure I was successful. "I hope they go well."

"Thanks. Me, too. Home game on Saturday, too. Busy week. I might be back at school on Friday."

Ugh. Mom had arranged her schedule with both work and Uncle Drew so we could leave Friday morning and I could have a practice session on the actual ice where my test would take place. "I won't be there on Friday."

A look of disappointment crossed his face, but he quickly brightened. "Oh, right! Your test. Are you all ready? Getting excited?"

Just talking about it made me slightly queasy. I was far from ready. "I'm not sure if 'excited' is the right word."

Pierce took my hand and gave it a squeeze. It didn't completely remove my nerves, but it helped. "Try to relax. Your coach wouldn't set you up for failure. She wouldn't ask you to do something you can't do. You got this. You just need to believe it."

Easier said than done, but I would try.

Up ahead, Carson came to a stop at the front doors. He didn't bust through like most kids would have, happy for the few seconds of independence. Instead, he looked back at his brother and waited until we got a few feet closer, inside some invisible radius that only Carson could see, then he stepped outside. Pierce was Carson's walking, talking security blanket. Despite his cocky exterior, Pierce really was a good guy. Maybe leaving my name off the list of potential Superfan01 people hadn't been intentional. After all, I hadn't given him any reason to suspect otherwise. Maybe I needed to. To own up to who I was. Who I *really* was. My stomach churned just as much as it had when I thought about my test.

"Pierce?"

"Yeah?"

We came to a stop near the first row of cars in the parking lot, where I'd have to turn left to get to my car and he'd have to turn right to get to his. Ahead of us, Carson stopped, too, reaching the end of that invisible radius.

All I had to do was own up to my online account. He liked her. He liked *me*. It would be okay. "I…"

After a few seconds, he frowned and asked, "You…?"

I couldn't. It was too embarrassing. I'd gotten in too far and he'd think I was crazy and if he knew how much I knew about hockey, I'd have to talk about my dad and nope. I couldn't do any of that. "I'll text you," I said instead. "Good luck. With your games."

"Pierce! Legos!" Carson called.

Pierce smiled and rolled his eyes. "Duty calls."

He leaned in and kissed me, a soft, sweet surprise to which Carson yelled, "Ew! You kissed a girl!" and made us both laugh.

He tucked a strand of hair that had fallen out of my bun behind my ear, smiled at me once more, and then turned to his brother. "Yeah, yeah. Okay, Lego Boy. Let's go."

I watched them leave, listening to Carson's happy chatter. My cheeks were still flushed, partly from that kiss, but mostly from embarrassment. As I took a deep breath and walked to my car, I had no clue what I was going to do.

Chapter Eighteen

She was going to tell me *something* before we left the rink. When she chickened out, I almost out and out asked her if she was Superfan01. Helped her out. But there was that one percent chance that she *wasn't* Superfan01, and if she wasn't, that could get really awkward really quickly. But as I scrolled through our NTDP private messages for the thousandth time, I knew it *had* to be her. I just needed her to own up to it.

PierceMiller: *Game day tomorrow…any advice for me?*

As soon as I clicked send, the hotel bathroom door opened, releasing a cloud of steam and the scent of whatever soap Luke Jackson had used. Jackson was my roommate for this trip, which was good. He liked the same music as me, didn't snore, and didn't try to have FaceTime sex with his girlfriend while I was in the room, which unfortunately was not something I could say about all of my teammates.

"Damn, man. Did you save any hot water for me?"

Jackson flopped down on his bed across the room. "Nah, not one drop."

"Asshole," I said, but didn't really mean it. I glanced at the clock. It was late. Well past Coach's curfew, after which we had to be locked in our hotel rooms or risk being benched for at least a game or two. Maybe Lia was already asleep. But then my phone lit up with a message notification.

Superfan01: *Hmm…you're in Canada, right? Distract them with a moose and by saying "eh" a lot?*

"Talking to the figure skater?" Jackson asked as he opened his own laptop.

"Absolutely not," I said. "Doing homework."

"You always grin like an idiot while doing homework?"

I laughed and stopped typing long enough to flip Jackson off.

PierceMiller: *Wow, my playing has gotten bad enough to need moose distractions? TBH, I'm kind of proud.*

Superfan01: *You should be.*

Superfan01: *Serious advice? Relax. Have fun. Isn't that why you play hockey?*

I really wanted to suggest that she take her own advice, but then I started thinking about her question. I looked over at Jackson, who was watching a video on his computer, but not loud enough that I could figure out what it was. "Hey, is hockey still fun?"

He glanced at me before turning back to the screen. "Hell yeah, man. The rush when you hit the ice? The adrenaline when there's a puck headed your way? It's fun."

I grunted and let my fingers linger over the keys, not typing anything.

Jackson looked over at me again. "Is it not fun for you?"

I considered. It always had been fun. Especially when I played for the school team with Robbie. When I was on top of my game and better than everyone who crossed my path. It was even fun when I started playing with NTDP—the excitement, the challenge, all of the press and the news and the attention. But that all felt like such a long time ago. "I don't know. I mean, I think so? I still love being on the ice. Love traveling and practicing and playing with you and the guys. But…"

"But it's a lot less fun when you're playing like crap and losing every single game and everyone is blaming it on you."

Guilt twisted in my gut. "I mean, when you put it like that, how could I *not* see that as fun?"

Jackson set his laptop aside and drew one knee up to his chest. "Sorry. Not what I meant. I just get it, you know? Of course it's not as fun when it's not going well. Going well is some of the best parts. Like last year." He grinned. "Annihilating that last team in the championship? That was fun."

It had been. The whole team had poured onto the ice and tackled Jackson, who had shut out the other team while NTDP scored goal after goal. We'd dumped an icy bucket of Gatorade on our coach's head on his way to the locker room. We'd been given trophies in front of cheering fans.

It didn't feel like any of that was going to happen this year. Not if I didn't turn things around. The pressure wasn't fun. And I was having a hard time separating the pressure from the game.

"There's still time," Jackson said. "We aren't out of the running. We just need to turn things around."

"*I* need to turn things around," I said.

"No, *we*," he said. "We're a team. You have a rough night, we need to have your back."

"And what about if I have a bad season?"

Jackson raised an eyebrow. "Then we need to get very, very drunk to forget about it."

I laughed. "Now *that* would be fun."

"Damn straight," Jackson said, sitting back and picking up his laptop again.

PierceMiller: *Yeah. Fun is why I play. It's just more fun when I don't suck and we win.*

Superfan01: *Have fun first. The winning will follow.*

God, I wanted her to be Lia. Or really, even though I was 99 percent sure she *was* Lia, I wanted her to confirm it so we could get rid of the dual identities. So she could be the one girl I liked instead of two. I rubbed my thumb over my jaw—I really needed to shave—before typing a question into the PM window. I hit send before I could change my mind.

PierceMiller: *Who are you?*

Superfan01: *I'm a super fan. Superfan01, to be exact.*

PierceMiller: *No, outside the internet. Who are you for real?*

It took a while for her to respond. Jackson showed me another video he was watching, some dumb stunt involving a skateboard, a roof, and a zip line, but my attention was more on my phone than anything. Waiting for her to respond. Waiting for my suspicions to be confirmed. My phone did light up for a second, but only with a text from my mom asking if I'd seen

Caron's blanket. He was much too old for a blanket, and only used it when he was at home, but he must have been feeling pretty rough if he was asking for it. He always did worse when I was traveling. I told her to check my closet, which was where he'd hidden it a few days ago during a meltdown. Sure enough, it was there. I was happy to help my family, but those texts weren't the phone notification I wanted. Finally, when Jackson was laughing his head off at the video's ending, the response I wanted came through.

Superfan01: *Who says I'm anyone other than that? Not everyone is two different people, like you.*

That caught me completely off-guard. Not only was it not the confirmation I was looking for, but she'd also flipped this on me. How had that happened?

PierceMiller: *Wait, wait. What do you mean? I'm not two different people. I'm Pierce Miller in real life and PierceMiller on the internet.*

The next response came a lot quicker.

Superfan01: *Maybe, but you're different when you're talking to me than you are when you're talking to other fans on the forum or talking to reporters or anything like that. With those, you're still confident. Still cocky. With me, you're more real. Pierce Miller is not the same as PierceMiller. Not from where I'm standing.*

She had a point. But she still hadn't told me who she was, or even where it was that she was standing.

Jackson, still laughing a little, closed his laptop. "Man, that shit is hilarious." He set his computer on the nightstand, turned off the lamp over his bed, and yawned. "You staying up?"

"Maybe just for a few more minutes," I said. "Will that bother you?"

"You know me. I'll be passed out cold in a few minutes."

It was true. Jackson slept like the dead no matter what was going on. There were numerous Instagram photos of him asleep on buses and airplanes and even on the bench in the middle of an NTDP game last season when he was nursing an injury and one of the backup goalies was in for him. But I turned off the lamp on my side of the bed anyway. The laptop cast a faint blue glow around the room. "Good night," I said.

"Night."

I turned my attention back to my laptop.

PierceMiller: *Maybe you're right. Maybe we'll have to meet in person sometime so you can see what I'm really like.*

Superfan01: *Maybe.*

Crap. If she was Lia, she wouldn't be willing to even consider meeting me in person, would she? I had to be right, but I was so afraid of being wrong.

Superfan01: *For now, I have to get some sleep. Good night, you Canuck hockey lover, you. Both of you.*

Despite my frustration and confusion, I smiled.

PierceMiller: *Good night, Superfan01 who may or may not exist outside of the internet. Talk to you soon.*

Chapter Nineteen

Lia

"Texting your boyfriend?" Adam plopped down on the couch next to me. Mom was working until seven, so I was in charge of my brother until she got home.

"No," I said quickly, even though I *was* texting back and forth with Pierce. Things weren't going so well in Canada. The team had lost their first game, and Pierce had played terribly. Apparently he hadn't listened to the "just have fun" conversation with Superfan01. Or even if he had, it hadn't been enough.

Adam looked over at my phone before I could pull it out of range of his gaze. "Yes, you are. You're texting Pierce."

I rolled my eyes before thumbing out a response to Pierce's question about how school was going without him. "He's not my boyfriend."

Adam tapped his own phone against his knee. "Do you know what guys hate even more than having the 'are we doing this relationship thing' conversation? Girls who refuse to have the 'are we doing this relationship thing' conversation.

It makes you seem insecure."

It stung because it was a little bit true. But Adam didn't need to know that. "You have no clue what you're talking about. You're like ten years old."

"I'm almost sixteen and mature for my age."

It took a lot to make me laugh so hard I snorted, but Adam and "mature" in the same sentence was enough to do it. "Yeah, right," I said, and continued laughing.

To make it even worse, Adam looked completely confused. "What's so funny? I *am* mature. That's why the ladies like me so much more than the rest of the punk kids at our school."

Oh God. *The ladies*. He was killing me. I was laughing so hard I could hardly breathe. Adam got in so much trouble he had to be constantly babysat by his mom, sister, or uncle, and he thought of himself as a ladies man? The kid had so much to learn...

"Quit laughing," Adam said. "I'm more mature than you. You won't even ask the guy you're swapping spit with if you're going out or whatever."

I struggled to compose myself. "Okay. Okay. You're right," I said, even though he absolutely wasn't. "You're mature."

He tossed a throw pillow at me. "Now you're just full of shit."

I deflected the shot. "Am not. I'm just admitting I was wrong. Now if you'll excuse me, sir, I'm going to put the laundry in the dryer." At least I waited until I was out of the room to start laughing again. As I switched the load of whites from the washing machine to the dryer, I thought of all the things that would happen before Adam matured: hell freezing over, pigs flying, Pierce winning another NTPD game. I winced and turned on the dryer. Okay, maybe that last one was a bit much. But still.

I managed to stop laughing by the time I walked back into the living room. Adam was sitting on the couch, long legs propped up on the coffee table, a textbook and notebook open in his lap. I froze. "What are you doing?"

"Homework."

But that couldn't be right. I hadn't had to argue with him or attempt to bribe him or threaten him with what would happen if Mom got home and his homework wasn't done. In other words, I hadn't had to do the things I'd had to do every other day for at least the past however many years to get him to do his schoolwork. "Why?"

He didn't even look up at me. "Because I'm supposed to learn things and get smarter. It's kind of my job."

"Right, but…" Wait. Why was I arguing with him about this? Even if I was confused about his motives and slightly suspicious about the fact that they might not be pure, I could still enjoy the rewards. Maybe he wanted something from Mom. Maybe he wanted me to tell her exactly how awesome and hard working he'd been. This was such a nice change from the ordinary that I might actually be willing to do it. "Good. That's good. Keep up the good work."

I flopped back onto my spot on the couch. My phone lit up with a text from Pierce.

Pierce: *Aren't you seeing someone else, too?*

Wait. What? That had nothing to do with the conversation we'd been having a minute ago about the words Canadians put the extra "u" in. Why was he talking about seeing people? I opened my text messages and scrolled up a little ways. There was the last message I sent him…except it wasn't the last message I sent him.

I whirled around to face Adam. "What the hell did you do?"

He studied my reaction with a smirk on his face, obviously no longer interested in his homework. "What? I did you a favor. Now you don't have to worry about having the conversation. You're having it. What did he say?"

I didn't realize my hands had started shaking until I tried to read the texts.

Pierce: *Color is just so much more exotic than color.*

Pierce: *Crap! I meant colour. Damn American autocorrect.*

Lia: *So, me and you. Are we official? Or just casual?*

I clenched the phone so hard the case started to creak in protest. I glared at Adam. "What the hell were you thinking? This is so wrong. *So* wrong."

Adam said something, but I was too upset to listen, so I kept reading.

Pierce: *Well…I was going to talk to you about this in person, but since you asked, I am kind of seeing someone else.*

Pierce: *Aren't you seeing someone else, too?*

All of the blood drained out of my face. I stopped hearing whatever Adam was saying. Pierce was seeing someone else. Was he crazy? No, I wasn't seeing anyone else! I only liked *him*. Going out with two guys at once wasn't something I did!

But going out with two girls at once was something Pierce did.

Which I'd known all along. But I let myself think that I could be different. That *he* could be different. How could I have been so wrong?

"Lia?" Adam's voice broke into my thoughts. "Are you okay?"

The concerned look on his face let me know just how bad

I must look. Adam was never concerned. About anything.

"He's seeing someone else," I said. The words sounded like they belonged to someone else. I wished they did.

"Shit. Well, at least now you know, right? You're not dragging it out or anything?"

I wanted to continue being angry at Adam. To tear him apart for getting into my phone and sticking his nose where it didn't belong. The anger would be so much easier than this devastation. How could I have let myself get involved with Pierce Miller? How could I have been so stupid?

I mumbled something about going upstairs. When I got there, I collapsed onto my bed and stared at the ceiling. A single tear slid down my cheek, landing somewhere in my hair. My phone, which I didn't even realize was still in my hand, buzzed with a new text message. It took a minute for me to gather my courage and look at the screen.

Pierce: *Lia? Hello?*

I stared at the message until the screen went black. Maybe we should have had this conversation sooner. Maybe it wasn't fair of me to be upset with Pierce when we hadn't had this conversation, so he didn't know he was doing anything wrong. But it *was* wrong. Never in a million years could I imagine spending time with Pierce, kissing him, getting close to him, and then kissing someone else. The fact that he could, that I was just another girl, when I'd thought I meant something to him, made me feel sick.

I unlocked my phone.

Lia: *No, I'm not seeing anyone else. Or at least I wasn't. Bye, Pierce.*

Then I went into my settings, blocked Pierce's number, and wished it were that easy to block the pain.

Chapter Twenty

"How's the arm?" Coach asked, taking the seat next to mine a few minutes into our drive. Usually he sat in the bus's front row, right behind the driver where he didn't have to deal with all of us, so obviously this seat meant he wanted to chat. Fantastic.

Wordlessly, I held out my left arm for him. I'd taken a nasty hit during one of the rare moments I'd been on the ice, before Coach had benched me the rest of the game. The hit had wrenched my elbow, causing a throbbing pain. It was a stupid hit, one that I should have been able to avoid, but I hadn't. Coach manipulated my arm, testing the flexion and extension. I stifled a wince of pain. It hurt, but I could tell it wasn't anything serious.

"Did you ice it?" Coach asked.

"Yeah."

"Keep icing it for twenty-four hours, then heat."

I grunted, hoping that was all, that he'd come over to

check on my injury and would now return to his seat, but no dice. He did glance over his shoulder, but only long enough to yell, "Hey. Sit down, you hooligans. You fall and break a bone on the bus, you're benched the rest of the season."

This direction was met with the usual protesting and complaining, but it did quiet down. I pulled out my phone. No texts from Lia. No NTDP forum messages from Superfan01. No surprise.

Lia had her chance to be honest with me. It was right there in front of her. And yeah, I'd wanted to have the conversation in person, but between our two travel schedules, I had no clue when I'd get to see her again. Her question was out of the blue, but I was glad she asked it. I was glad she gave me the opportunity to put it all out there. To get her to admit who she really was. Yes, I was seeing someone else, but so was she, and it was time to be real about that.

But then she'd said she *wasn't* seeing anyone else. She hadn't confessed. When she asked that question, I *knew* she was going to tell me that Superfan01 was Lia and Lia was Superfan01, but she didn't. Did she really think I was that stupid? And if she could lie to me about that online relationship, leave out who her father was, what else could she lie to me about?

Damn if she hadn't pulled all of this on game day. And damn if I couldn't stop thinking about it while I was on the ice.

"Put that away," Coach said, swatting at my phone. "We're not done here."

Great. I put the phone away.

"So," he said, with a sigh that let me know he didn't want to have whatever conversation was about to happen just as much as I didn't want to have it. "I talked to Scott Butler."

One of the Red Wings's scouts. This couldn't be going anywhere good. "And?"

"And he's a little disappointed in your performance this

season."

I tugged on a loose thread on the back of the seat in front of me. "Yeah, well that makes two of us."

"He's coming to the game on Saturday."

My stomach clenched. When he came last time, I was excited. I was on top of my game. I was ready to show him what I could do. Now I wasn't sure what I possibly had to show him that would be worth anything. "Great."

"Normally after a game like today, your ass would be sitting the bench on Saturday. Maybe even next week."

I nodded. There was nothing I could say to defend myself. But I sensed a "but" coming.

"But he needs to see you play again. And I can't deny you that opportunity. So you're going to play. But I want you to know this is your last shot."

I understood his meaning. Last shot with the Wings. Last shot with the team itself. Last shot at my future. "Yes, sir."

"You know what I think?" Coach asked, but didn't wait for me to continue. "I think you've gotten this far on who you are. Your natural talent. Your skills. Your good coaches and teachers along the way. I think you've never really had to fight for anything."

Never had to fight for anything? Was he serious? How did he think I'd gotten this far? "But Coach, I—"

"Don't argue," Coach said. "Just listen. I think, for whatever reason, your natural talent and skills are failing you. It happens to everyone at one point or another. But the difference between everyone and the greats is that the greats know how to fight. Despite the circumstances, despite the pressure, despite whatever is going on, they fight. I think you have to fight for what you want. Not just play hard. Not just work hard. I know you do all that. But you have to really fight for what you want."

I let out a long sigh. "And how am I supposed to do that?"

Coach patted my shoulder, and I winced when it jostled my elbow. "That, you're going to have to figure out for yourself. You've got two days."

Then he was gone, back to the safety at the front of the bus.

Great talk, Coach.

Chapter Twenty-One

Lia

There was a knock on my bedroom door. "Embry?" I asked. If it was my brother, I might not be able to see him without killing him right now.

"Yeah. It's me."

"Come in," I said, wiping at my eyes and hoping the mascara smears weren't too terrible. Not that Embry would care.

"Hey," she said as she opened the door. It was a sympathetic "hey," a gentle one, like I was fragile and might break at any second. I'd texted her to tell her what had happened, and she had insisted on coming over immediately. She'd changed out of the outfit she'd been wearing at school and was in a pair of leggings and a long T-shirt.

"Hey," I said back. "Did my brother let you in?" With my sudden lack of supervision, I wouldn't be shocked if he'd up and left, off to make trouble somewhere else, but Mom would just have to understand.

"Yeah. He's on the couch, playing on his phone."

"Asshole," I said, then quickly added, "him, not you."

Embry nudged me over so she could sit next to me on the bed. "Yeah, so your texts were kind of confusing. Can you go back to the beginning? Tell me exactly what happened?" She adjusted my pillow behind her back, then folded her hands in her lap, ready to listen.

I took a deep breath and told her everything, answering her clarifying questions when I got emotional again and talked so fast my words got jumbled and I skipped details she needed.

When I finished, she said, "Oh, Lia. I'm so, so sorry."

I wiped at my eyes, refusing to let another tear fall over freaking Pierce Miller. "It's not your fault."

"I know, but I still feel bad. I hate seeing you hurt, and I feel like I encouraged this whole thing."

"You didn't. It was my own fault."

"No, it was *his* fault."

I snorted. "True."

"It's kind of weird, though. I know he hasn't been at school this week, but last week I didn't see him with anyone new. Pierce has never been one to keep his relationships quiet, except maybe with you. And I think that was only because your paths didn't really cross. I wonder who this new girl is."

"Maybe he's over all of the girls at Troy Prep and has had to look elsewhere. One of his adoring fans."

"Maybe. So what now?"

"I don't know. I blocked his number. I just don't even want to deal with him right now."

"What about the whole NTDP forum thing? Are you still talking to him there?"

Actually, I hadn't heard from PierceMiller in a few days, and definitely not since I found out he was seeing someone else. "Nope. Apparently this new girl is enough to distract him from that, too."

"You really liked him, didn't you?"

A pang of regret at her use of the past tense struck hard and fast. I had liked him. I liked the rush that came with every touch. Every conversation. I liked the way he made me feel important. Made me feel confident. "Yeah. And I know it's crazy because I'm so incredibly pissed at him, but I kind of think I still like him." I sighed. "I wonder how long it will take before that goes away?"

"It's not crazy." She picked at a hangnail on her left thumb. "And I know you're pissed, but did you talk to him? I mean maybe he's less serious with that girl than he is with you. Maybe he'd break it off with whoever she is to be with you if you just talk to him and tell him that's what you want."

Tears filled my eyes again, some combination of self-pity and self-hatred. "Yeah, right. Why in the world would he choose me over anyone else?"

"Because you're awesome," Embry said immediately, turning to look at me. "Don't you know that? You're kind and smart and talented and pretty, and he'd be crazy *not* to choose you."

Another tear spilled down my cheek before I could catch it. "You have to say that. You're my friend."

"No, I *get* to say that because you're my friend."

That made me cry even harder. Embry alternated between patting my arm and smoothing my hair until I calmed down. "I don't want to talk to him," I said. My voice sounded like it did when I had a cold. "What if he says he's choosing the other girl?"

"Then you won't be any worse off than you are right now. And at least you'll know."

"I'll be mortified."

"Why? If he doesn't choose you, that's his loss. It's not like you see him at school often anyway."

"Yeah, but I have to see him at the workshop at the rink."
Oh God. I hadn't even thought about the workshop until the
words were out of my mouth. My test had gotten me out of
the workshop this weekend, but I was going to have to see him
the next week. I couldn't miss two weeks in a row. I couldn't
do that to Mr. Kozlov.

"All the more reason to talk to him."

I sighed. "I guess."

"Now," Embry stood and cracked her knuckles. "It's time
to have a chat with that brother of yours."

"Don't make him bleed. It'll just stain the carpet and we'll
have to clean it up."

"Oh, Adam," Embry called as she walked down the stairs.
She wouldn't really hit him. I didn't think.

I hesitated just inside my bedroom door before following.
I unlocked my phone. I'd already changed my pass code, since
apparently using Pierce's hockey number twice had been a
little too easy for my brother to figure out. There was only one
number in my list of blocked numbers. I let my finger hover
over the button to un-block it, but then chickened out and hit
the home screen before heading downstairs.

Embry was right. I needed to talk to him. But I wasn't
ready yet, and I wasn't sure when I would be. That would take
confidence I wasn't sure I had.

Chapter Twenty-Two

It was before eight a.m. on Saturday morning, and I couldn't sleep. I hadn't fallen asleep until after two a.m., so there was absolutely zero reason I should be awake. I needed sleep to have any hope of playing well today. Instead, I was on my tablet, watching hockey videos. Of my opponents, of myself, of the greats. Trying to see what Coach was talking about. What it looked like to fight for a win. I saw talent in the videos—the puck skills and the footwork and the skating speed—all of that seemed to be what made them win. I'd been thinking about it for two days, and I still had no idea what Coach was talking about.

As one YouTube video ended, another one started before I could think of another set of search keywords that might get me to what I was looking for. The new video caught my attention, though. It was a clip from an old Red Wings game, back in the days of Steve Ziegler. The Wings were down two to one with less than a minute in the third period.

"Looks like the Wings are pulling their goalie in a last-ditch effort to stay in the game," the announcer said. The sound was rough because the video was so old, but it was still understandable. "And I don't believe it, but they're putting Ziegler back in the game as the sixth man."

On the screen, I watched as Lia's dad jumped over the boards and onto the ice the second their goalie hit the bench.

"After the night he's had, I'm not sure that's the best move," another announcer chimed in. "The Wings can't afford a mistake, and all he's done so far is make mistakes."

"Uncharacteristic night for Ziegler, but now he gets the puck. He heads behind the net, but Robertson is right behind him, and oh! Robertson steals the puck away."

I winced at the rookie mistake. Underneath the announcer's voice, I heard the outraged yells of the Wings' fans. But Ziegler didn't give up. He didn't let one of the other five guys on the ice pick up his slack. No, he pushed harder and faster than should have been humanly possible and caught back up to Robertson.

"Ziegler checks Robertson, who passes the puck to Kirchoff, but I don't believe it! Ziegler's there again! He grabs the puck and…"

Fell. Ziegler tripped over nothing and face-planted in the middle of the ice. The clock in the corner of the screen counted down. Five…four…three… The other Wings players scrambled to get back to Ziegler, who had taken the puck down with him, but they weren't going to get there in time. Ziegler, still on his stomach, used the grip-end of his stick in a way I'm sure had never been used before and would never be used again, and smacked the puck toward the goal. By the time the Rangers' goalie figured out what was happening, it was too late. The puck was in the net. The arena roared with applause. Ziegler's teammates collapsed on top of him. The video ended.

I had no idea if the Wings went on to win or lose that game. If they went into overtime or a shootout. But it didn't matter. Ziegler had shown me what I needed to see. He didn't use his talent to score that goal. The mistakes he made were so similar to the ones I'd been making lately. Maybe even worse. But he fought for that goal. He fought for what he wanted. Lia's dad had shown me what that looked like so I could do the same.

Lia.

I needed to fight for what I wanted. And what I really wanted was her.

I scrambled out of bed and got ready as quickly as possible. Despite my lack of sleep, I wasn't tired. I ran down the stairs two at a time and into the kitchen, where my parents and brother were already awake.

"Good morning, Pierce," my mom said before taking a sip from her cup of coffee.

"Pierce didn't sleep all day!" Carson cheered. "Want to build Legos with me?"

"Later, Bub. I promise," I said, grabbing my car keys from the kitchen counter where I'd left them last night.

"Where are you going?" Dad asked.

"I have to go talk to Lia."

"Isn't it a bit early for that? Why don't you just text her?"

Texting wasn't making a shot from my belly in the middle of the ice, but my dad wouldn't understand that. "I need to talk to her in person. I'll be back."

Before my family could argue or attempt to drag me into Lego building, I rushed out the door, got in the car, put the key in the ignition…and promptly realized I had no clue where I was going. Shit.

I called Lia, but it only rang once before going straight to voicemail. I tried again, but got the same result. So I threw the car in reverse and headed in the direction of someone who

I knew would have Lia's address. When I reached the rink, I left the car running in a no parking zone and prayed none of the early morning hockey moms would call the cops on me. I ran inside. Mr. Kozlov was at the front desk, sorting through a stack of mail.

"Pierce Miller!" he said, face brightening when he saw me. "You are early with the worms."

I knew the saying he was going for but didn't bother correcting him. "I need Lia's address."

Confusion crossed Mr. Kozlov's face. "The Lia Bailey? Why?"

"Because I need to talk to her. Some things got messed up between us, and I need to fix them."

Mr. Kozlov considered this for a minute before nodding. "Okay. I will give it to you." He reached under the desk and pulled out a box filled to the top with papers. Most looked like old receipts, but it was impossible to tell because there was absolutely zero organization.

Oh God, this was going to take forever.

"It is in here. I know right where it is," he said as he started filtering through.

I didn't believe him.

But then he said "Ah-ha," like he did, in fact, know where it was the whole time. He handed over the paper—a receipt for freestyle ice time—and I removed my phone to put the address into my GPS.

"Thanks, Mr. Kozlov. You're the best."

I took off before he could respond and followed the directions to Lia's house. The GPS said it would take ten minutes to get there, but my lead foot ensured that it took about five. I pulled in the driveway and glanced at the clock. Good, it was after eight o'clock. I didn't have to feel quite as bad about knocking on her door so early.

But as I ran up to the porch, I saw that knocking wasn't

going to be necessary. Lia's brother was asleep on the front porch swing in a sleeping bag, pillow tucked awkwardly under his neck. I would have thought I had the wrong house, but I recognized him from the "kissing in the ice arena parking lot" thing. What the hell?

I cleared my throat. When that didn't wake him, I said, "Hey."

He stirred, stretched, winced at the awkward angle of his neck, and opened his eyes.

"What are you doing here?" he asked, voice slightly hoarse.

"I could ask you the same thing," I said, motioning to the awkward sleeping arrangement.

The brother nodded to the front door, where I noticed a note that had been duct taped to the glass. "My uncle's in charge, and he's an asshole."

Adam,

Congratulations! You missed curfew. Now you get to spend the night out here. I've been nice enough to provide a sleeping bag and a bottle of water. Don't bother knocking. I'll see you in the morning.

Love,
Uncle Drew

"Aren't you a bit young to be breaking curfew?" I asked.

"Aren't you a bit of a douchebag to be showing your face here?" he countered.

Okay, so clearly Adam knew about the argument with Lia. "That's what I'm here for. To talk to her. To apologize."

At that moment, the front door opened. Lia's uncle, whom I also recognized from the ice arena parking lot, opened the door, smile on his face. Cup of coffee in his hand. He looked so much like his brother. How had I missed that before?

"I thought I heard voices out here," he said. "Why, good morning, Adam! Nice of you to make it home. Too bad it wasn't before curfew. Hope you had a good night outside."

Adam rubbed his eyes and grumbled something unintelligible about child protective services.

Drew turned to me. "Good morning. What can I help you with?"

"I'm here to talk to Lia," I said.

"She's not here. She and her mom are in Ohio. That's why I'm here with this one." He nodded to Adam.

Ohio. Her skating test. *Shit.* How could I have forgotten? In the midst of our argument, I hadn't even gotten to tell her good luck. What kind of crappy person was I? Things just got a hell of a lot more complicated, but I wasn't about to give up. "Where in Ohio?"

Drew crossed his arms over his chest. "Why do you want to know?"

Adam used this distraction to sneak behind Drew into the house, like he wasn't sure he'd be let in any other way. Drew either didn't see it or didn't stop it.

"I need to talk to her."

Drew studied me like I was something disgusting on the bottom of his shoe. "Right now? When she's out of state taking a test? Why don't you just text her?"

I sighed. "She's not answering my texts. Or my calls. Look, I messed up. I need to explain some things to her. Apologize to her. Show her that I'm serious. What better way to do that than by driving to Ohio to support her, right?"

He studied me another full minute. It was just long enough for me to convince myself that he was going to say no. To tell me to turn around and get the hell out of here. But then he stepped back into the house and nodded for me to follow. "I think I saw some registration paperwork on the fridge."

I followed him inside. My attention was immediately

drawn to a large framed collage. It was the best of Steve Ziegler in photographs. It had to hurt Lia to see that every day. I forced myself away from it and walked into the kitchen. Adam was standing at the counter, eating a bowl of cereal, and Drew was studying a piece of paper.

"Columbus," Drew said. "The rink right downtown."

I checked a clock on the microwave and did the math. I could make it there in about three hours. It would be cutting it close. By the time I got there, talked to her, watched her skate, and drove back, it might be time for my game to start. But I'd taken the easy way out for too long. It wasn't working out for me. I was going to go for it.

"Thank you," I said, and turned to rush to my car, but then a thought crossed my mind. There was one problem. A big one. I turned back around and looked to Adam. "Do you know how to ice skate?"

He swallowed his bite of cereal. "Um, do you know who my dad was?"

Perfect. I reached for my wallet. "I need a favor."

Chapter Twenty-Three

Lia

My mom nudged my shoulder. "You good?"

I nodded, but only because if I shook my head, she'd asked me what was wrong, and if I opened my mouth to answer her, there was a good chance I'd throw up. There were two more skaters, then it would be my turn in front of the judges. The next skater was a guy. I crossed my fingers and willed him to do better than the girl before him, who'd left the ice in tears. I was terrified I'd be the one leaving the ice in tears soon.

As the music started, motion near the rink's entrance caught my eye. Someone had walked in. Weird. It almost looked like Pierce. God, I really needed to get him out of my brain. But as the guy walked closer, scanning the rows of bleachers, I realized the guy didn't just *look like* Pierce. He *was* Pierce. What in the world was Pierce doing in Ohio?

"Be right back," I mumbled to my mom, then walked down the bleachers, almost tripping on my blade guards. Not a good sign that I could barely *walk* in my skates.

The second Pierce saw me, he motioned to the arena doors, away from the bleachers. I followed him so we could talk without disrupting anyone else. Before I could say a word, he took a quick look at me from head to toe. I was wearing the same plum-colored lacy skating dress I'd worn when I'd passed the junior test. My hair was in a sleek bun, and I was wearing my skate-covering tights that made my legs appear extra long.

"You look amazing," he said.

My knees went a little weak, and I hated myself for it. Yeah, Pierce Miller thought I was pretty, but what did that matter? He was an asshole. I had the proof. "What are you doing here?" I asked as I crossed my arms over my stomach.

"I wanted to talk to you. Needed to talk to you."

"Yeah, well I'm kind of busy." I nodded toward the ice. The guy's program was winding down. One skater left before me. It was so tempting to run out the arena doors and never look back.

"I know."

I waited for him to continue, but he didn't. "Well? Tic tock."

He hesitated. "Now? You want to do this right before you get on the ice?"

He'd already told me he was seeing someone else. Already told me everything I needed to hear. I just wanted to get whatever this was over with. "Yes."

He sighed and ran a hand through his hair, making a couple of the curls stand on end. Then he shifted from foot to foot but still didn't say anything. It was almost like he was nervous. I'd never seen Pierce nervous before.

"So, you're *sure* you're not seeing anyone else?" he finally blurted out.

Anger spiked fast and hard, overpowering my nerves. "Seriously? How dare you accuse me of seeing someone else when you said yourself *you're* seeing someone else! Double standard much? You're allowed to see someone else when I'm not? I can't believe you drove all the way out here to ask me that. You're an asshole."

He held both hands out, fingers spread, palms down. "Whoa, whoa. Lia. Calm down. You've got this all wrong."

"No, I don't," I said, loud enough that a few spectators glanced our direction. I lowered my volume, but not my intensity. "I can't believe you'd even…" I shook my head. I was wasting my breath. "You know what? Why do you even care? You've got someone else. Go be with her. You've got tons of girls throwing themselves at you. What do you need with me? You've got other girls like Superfan01. She's great, right? Mysterious? Confident? Guess what, Pierce. She's me."

"I know."

I was about to continue on, to tell him to get the hell back to Michigan and leave me alone, but his lack of a reaction stopped me in my tracks. "You what?"

"I know. I've known for a while. When I said I was seeing someone else, I was trying to feel you out because I was 99 percent sure you were her…or, well, you were you, but I didn't want to mess anything up with you on the off one-percent chance it wasn't true. I wanted you to say the same. Hoped you'd say the same. But clearly that plan backfired. I screwed up. I'm really sorry."

I opened my mouth but had no clue what to say, so I stood there gaping like a fish.

"*You're* the only one I'm seeing," he said. "Both of you. All of you. Only you."

More gaping. Still no talking, until Pierce glanced over at the ice. "They called your name."

What? How had that happened? Oh crap. I wasn't ready. I couldn't do this. I started shaking, which was pretty terrible for balance.

"Lia," he said, and took my shaking hands in his. "You got this. Deep breaths. Relax. You can do this. There's nothing you're about to do out there you haven't done a million times already. I have faith in you. Have faith in yourself."

Tears stung the back of my eyes, but I nodded once. I turned toward the ice, but only made it a few steps away.

"Hey, Lia?"

I turned back.

"No matter what happens, your dad would be proud of you."

He knew. He knew everything. And he was still here.

I hoped he was right.

When I stepped off the ice, my mind was reeling. I had no clue how I'd done during the test. Miraculously, I hadn't frozen up. I hadn't fallen…I didn't think. I was pretty sure I'd done all my moves, but beyond that I knew nothing. I broke my non-negotiable rule by stepping off the ice without blade guards and rushed over to Pierce.

"You were amazing," he said, wide grin and dimples on his face. "No matter what happens, be proud of what you did out there."

But I didn't care how I'd done. "The workshop! You're missing the workshop!" I was still terribly out of breath. "And don't you have a game today? What time is your game?"

"Your brother is teaching the workshop for me."

My face, which had been warm from exertion, instantly cooled as all the blood left my cheeks. "What?"

Pierce laughed. "It's okay. I'm paying him, and he's getting a little help from your uncle and Mr. Kozlov. He seemed kind of excited about the responsibility. Maybe it will be good for him." He took my blade guards out of my hands and bent down to help me put them on.

"They'll never come back. The parents of those kids are going to riot and demand a refund and Mr. Kozlov is going to—"

"It'll be okay," Pierce said as he stood again. "Trust me. Trust Adam."

I put my palm to my forehead. There was too much going through my brain. "You knew. You knew who I was." On one level I was relieved, but I also felt so, so stupid. Having two identities was bad enough, but having Pierce *know* I had two identities when I didn't know? That was so much worse.

"I did."

"And you're not seeing anyone else."

"Not even a little bit."

In the stands behind us there was some cheering, but I ignored it. "And you drove three hours to tell me all of this."

He smiled. "Well, that and to do this." Then he cupped one hand under my chin, leaned down, and kissed me hard. It felt like it was our first kiss all over again, only better because there wasn't any hesitation. Despite our time apart, right here was where we belonged, with his arms holding me close and my lips locked on his, leaving me breathless for reasons that had nothing to do with skating. But it only took a second for my mind to start whirring again. I pushed back.

"Wait, wait," I said. "What about your game? What time is that? What time is it now?"

Before he could answer, people started filling the empty space around us, heading toward the rink's exit. Because I'd registered late, I'd been last to skate. They'd made announcements on who passed, and I completely missed it. Pierce and I inched closer together as the sea of people— mostly parents and coaches, some with skaters in tears, some grinning from ear to ear—split around us.

Suddenly Mom was hugging me from behind. "You did

it! You passed!"

It took a second for the words to register. I'd passed? The senior test? I turned to face her. "I passed?"

"You passed," Mom said. There were tears in her eyes. I knew those tears. They were the "I wish your dad were here" tears. Holy shit. I passed. I could go to regionals. Nationals. Worlds. The Olympics. And none of it had to be my dad's pie in the sky dream that died with him. It could be reality.

"I'm so proud of you," Pierce said, circling long fingers around my wrist, reminding me he was there. I turned back to him, and he hugged me tight. "I knew you could do it."

God, he smelled good. This *felt* good. I leaned in to the hug and savored what I'd missed.

"Hey, isn't that Pierce Miller?" someone asked.

"Can't be," someone else said, even though he was looking right at Pierce. "He has a game in Michigan this afternoon."

"Pierce?" my mom asked while the two fans walked away without realizing it really *was* Pierce. "What are you doing in Ohio? I thought you two were..."

Pierce released me, and I said, "We had some misunderstandings, but we're all good now."

Mom looked confused, but still happy. "Oh. Good."

"Four o'clock," Pierce said.

"What?" I asked.

"My game's at four o'clock. So I should probably go..."

I looked at the clock on the wall. *Shit.* "Pierce, it's almost one o'clock! You'll never make it!"

"Yes, I will," he said. "And if I don't, this was more important."

My cheeks warmed as Mom made a little "aw" sound. I turned to her. "Can I ride back with Pierce?"

Mom eyed Pierce, who was already digging his keys out of his pocket. "I don't know..."

"I've never gotten a ticket or been in an accident, if that

helps," he said.

"It does," I said. "Come on, Mom. Please." I had to see him through this. We'd been back together for fewer than five minutes. We couldn't just go our separate ways. Not now. Not yet. "Hey, remember that time I passed the senior test? This could totally be my reward."

The resigned look on her face let me know I'd played the right card. "Fine." She turned to Pierce. "I know you're in a hurry, but you must obey the speed limit at all times. And be *careful.*"

"I promise," Pierce said. Then he grabbed my hand and squeezed it. "Let's go."

He started running, but it only took two steps for me to remember running in skates wasn't the easiest thing to do. "Wait, my shoes!"

"We don't have time for shoes!" he said, but when he turned back to me, he wasn't angry or upset. There was a smile on his face and a sparkle in his eye. It seemed like he was ready for this adventure.

"Lia, catch," my mom said from behind me. When I turned, I was grateful for reflexes that allowed me to drop Pierce's hand and catch my skate bag before it hit me in the face. "Thanks," I said, looping it over my shoulder and running after Pierce as quickly as I could. He took my hand to help me along.

When we got in his car, he turned to me, still smiling. "Ready?"

I buckled my seat belt. "Let's do this."

Chapter Twenty-Four

"So, how's it feel to be the next senior skater?" I asked.

Lia zipped her bag and tossed it in the backseat. She'd changed out of her skates and into her shoes in the passenger seat. "It feels…weird."

"Good weird?"

"Yeah. Definitely good weird."

I set the cruise control at three over the speed limit. I figured that was close enough to count for the promise I made Lia's mom. But even if we didn't make it, I meant what I'd said. I'd made the right choice going to Ohio. I'd fought for what I wanted, and I'd gotten it. Gotten *her*.

"When are the next winter Olympics, three more years?" I asked. "That's enough time for you to get there, right?"

"There are still a lot of steps between now and then."

I rapidly approached a semi going too far under the speed limit for my taste and checked my blind spot before switching lanes. "But you can take all those steps, right?"

She was quiet for a second, so I glanced over at her. She was looking out the window. The sun hit her tights-covered thighs through the windshield at a sharp angle.

"I guess so," she said. "I think my problems getting here were mostly because of a mental block. I didn't think I could do it. I was afraid to fail."

"And now?" Out of the corner of my eye, I saw her smile at me.

"Now I've got a little more confidence. I'm going to try."

"Glad you learned from your alter ego."

"And from you."

She took her hair out of the tight bun it had been in. It fell over her shoulders in loose waves, and the sunlight glinted off it as we took a curve. Damn, she was gorgeous. "You're beautiful."

Immediately, she scoffed. "I don't know that I'm confident enough to believe that."

"You should believe it. Because you are." It was going to take time for her to see herself the way I saw her. That was okay. I had time. Well, not literally. Not actual time right now. But in general, I committed myself to making sure she believed it someday.

For now, I nodded to my phone. "What's our ETA?" I asked.

"Still three fifty-seven."

I nudged the speedometer to four over the speed limit. What Lia's mom didn't know wouldn't hurt her.

"So…how'd you know Superfan was me?" She almost sounded embarrassed talking about it.

"You slipped up a couple of times. I knew you went to Troy Prep, and I guess I had a feeling. Then once I figured out who your dad was, everything fell into place."

"And you weren't…disappointed?"

I snorted. "Are you kidding me? I *hoped* it was you. I had

no clue what I was going to do if it *wasn't* you."

"It was just easier," she said. Even though I was looking at the road, not at her, I could see out of the corner of my eye that she was talking with her hands, motioning to her cell phone. "Talking to you anonymously. It's just that the only interactions I'd had with you in person hadn't been great, and you were so—"

She cut herself off and I laughed. "Go ahead. You can say it."

"You were so confident," she said. "It was intimidating."

"Confident was not the word you were going to say the first time." I teased. I glanced at her and she grinned.

"Guilty, but I was going to follow it up by saying that then when I started talking to you, I expected our conversation to be as bad as it had been in person, but you were just so *nice*. And you made me feel important. Special."

"What can I say? I am nice and you are important and special."

"I didn't think so."

"I know. Which is why I liked talking to *you*. Both online and in person. Because I got to see this whole other side to you that I was pretty sure you didn't show anyone else. I do wish I would have admitted what I knew sooner. Then the misunderstanding thing wouldn't have happened."

"Not your fault. I should have just told you who I was, but then you would have wondered how I knew so much about hockey, and I would have had to tell you about my dad…"

"You don't talk about him to anyone, do you?"

"Not really. I know it's been a while, but it still hurts. And since our last names are different, it's easy to not talk about it."

I checked my surroundings to make sure there weren't any cops in sight and nudged my speed up a tiny bit higher. "Understandable. What's up with the last name thing, anyway?"

"He wasn't my father. Not by birth, anyway. Some other jerk I've never met was my birth father. My mom married my dad when I was almost two. Because of who he was, she kept her maiden name and gave it to me and my brother. It ended up working out for other reasons, though."

A thousand questions were racing through my mind. What was it like to be the daughter of a famous hockey player? Had she gotten to go to all the games? Go in the locker room? Touch the Stanley Cup? What was Steve Ziegler like when he wasn't on the ice? Had he taught her some of what he knew?

"Go ahead," she said, as if she could read my mind. "You can ask whatever you want to ask."

"You sure?"

She hesitated, but only for a second. "Yes."

The question that came out of my mouth wasn't any of the ones I'd initially thought of. "What was the deal with the necklace?"

"You noticed his necklace?"

My cheeks flushed a little. "To say I was a fan of your dad's would be an understatement." He'd constantly worn a necklace, but it was always tucked into whatever shirt or jersey he was wearing. I'd just noticed the thin silver chain around the back of his neck and seen him pulling it out and messing with it every once in a while, usually when a game was going really well or really terribly. I'd always had a feeling there was something to it.

"It's a silver four-leaf clover charm that belonged to his mom. He wore it for luck every single day." She reached under her skating dress.

Holy shit. She was wearing the necklace? How had I not noticed the familiar thin chain around the back of her neck?

Sure enough, she pulled out the too-long chain, and at the end was a small, silver four-leaf clover. "I guess it brought me some luck today." Before I could say anything else, she unclasped the chain, leaned over the console between us, and put it around my neck.

"Wait, what are you doing?" I asked, swerving back onto the road when I hit the rumble strips for a second.

She sat back against her own seat. "It brought me luck. Now it's going to bring you luck."

I reached up and felt the smooth metal. It was still warm from being pressed against her skin. Steve Ziegler had worn this necklace. Now I was wearing it. "You're sure?"

"Yes," she said, no hesitation this time.

"Thank you. And I guess it's the perfect day for it." I filled her in on what Coach had said, how I was pretty sure my present and future rested on today's game.

She groaned. "And you're going to be late because of me."

"Not late," I said. "Four minutes early. And remember. I made the choice because it was worth it. I had to go after what I wanted."

"Yeah, and I'm sure your coach will be thrilled with you walking in four minutes before puck drop."

"He'll live," I said.

Silence settled over us for the first time this trip. When I glanced over at her, she was looking out the window. We were in the middle of nowhere with nothing to see besides corn and cows. After a couple of minutes, she sighed.

"I haven't been to a game since that one."

Even though she hadn't said it, I knew which one she was talking about. The one during which her dad suffered the concussion that killed him. "Really?"

"Really. Not in person, anyway. It's different watching on TV or online. Being there in person is just too tense. So many memories. I guess I'm afraid I'll see the same thing happen to someone else."

The confession made me want to wrap my arms around

her and let her bury her head against my shoulder so I could protect her from seeing anything like that ever again. But that was no way to live. If I did that, she'd miss out on seeing the good things, too. "I can't even imagine. But terrible things can happen anywhere. Anytime. So can good things."

She seemed to consider that for a minute before nodding once. "Like the good things that are going to happen to you in today's game?"

I carefully tucked the charm under my shirt, just like Lia's dad always had. "Let's hope so. ETA?"

She picked my phone up out of the cup holder and checked the display. "Three fifty-five."

I took a deep breath. "Game on."

Chapter Twenty-Five

Lia

"You know where you're going, right?" Pierce asked from the backseat. Thankfully, he'd had enough forethought this morning to put his hockey bag in the car. Now he was changing into his pads, pants, and jersey. These last moments of our drive had been very carefully planned. We'd stopped in a parking lot just long enough for me to jump in the driver's seat and Pierce to jump in the backseat to change. The driver's seat was back so far I had to scoot up to reach the pedals, but there wasn't time to fix that now. Pierce's coach had already texted and called multiple times, probably trying to figure out where he was, but Pierce hadn't answered.

"Yep, I got it. I'm running every orange light I see, trying to get us there faster."

"Orange lights?"

Even though the jersey that he was pulling over his head muffled his voice, I knew what he was asking.

"You know, when the light's not red yet because that

would be illegal, but it's not really yellow anymore, either?"

He laughed. "I don't think that's a thing."

"It is when your game starts in," I checked the clock, "twenty-two minutes."

"Good point." He groaned. "I'm too tall to change in the backseat of a car. I'm going to pull a muscle and not be able to skate."

When I looked in the mirror, I tried to convince myself it was just to check for cars behind me. But there were no cars, and Pierce was fully dressed. Back in the front windshield, there was a traffic light that was definitely going to be on the red side of orange. "Hang on," I said right before I floored it.

"Whoa!" he said and laughed again as his bag went flying. "A little warning next time?"

"Sorry." But it was worth it because a few moments later, I was pulling in to the ice arena. I avoided the spectators looking for parking spaces and drove toward the front doors.

"You don't have to come watch the game. I understand." Pierce was sitting, now fully uniformed, one hand on his skates and the other on the door handle, ready to jump out the second I put the car in park.

"Don't worry about me," I said. "Just worry about playing like the Pierce Miller I know, okay?"

"On it."

I pulled up in front of the entrance and threw his car into park. He jumped out and I lowered my window. "Good luck," I yelled as he ran for the doors, but he only got a few steps away before he stopped and turned back. I thought he'd forgotten something, but instead he ran straight for me, stuck his head in the window, and kissed me. Hard. Kissed me. Kissed Superfan01. Kissed Steve Ziegler's daughter. Kissed all of me with all of him.

Against my better judgment, I pulled away and pushed him out the window. "Go," I said, laughing.

He smiled, letting his gaze linger on me for another second, then sprinted toward the entrance.

I found a parking space way at the back of the lot and walked inside. The smell of buttery popcorn was even stronger here than at The Ice House. I headed toward the ticket counter. I could do this. I could watch a hockey game. Pierce would be fine.

"Can I help you?" the ice arena employee asked, barely looking up from his cell phone.

I was about to tell him I'd take one ticket when something on the counter caught my eye. It was a bright yellow Post-it note with two words on it: Lia Bailey. The Post-it was stuck to a ticket. I bit my lip. "Is that…is this for me?"

The guy looked from his phone to the ticket to me. "Are you Lia Bailey?"

He looked me up and down once after he asked, and it was only then I realized I was still wearing my skating dress from this morning's test. At least I was in an ice arena, so I wasn't *completely* out of place. "Yes."

He shrugged. "Then it's yours. Enjoy the game."

I gingerly picked up the ticket and removed the note. On the back was a sentence that had obviously been written so quickly I could barely read it: *So you don't have to sit alone.*

Curious, I looked at the ticket and headed into the rink. It had a completely different vibe than a rink during a skating competition. It was louder. More crowded, with a sea of red, white, and blue USA Hockey support. And of course there about twenty times as many guys on the ice. I'd forgotten what this energy was like. And this was only about a tenth of what it had been at Joe Louis Arena, where my dad played.

When I located my row on the ticket, it was only a couple of rows off the ice. Before I could even find my seat number, I realized where I was going. Right around center ice, I recognized a familiar bright green pair of noise-canceling headphones. Carson. And Pierce's parents. Even in his rush to get to the game, he'd stopped long enough to make sure I had this ticket. That I wouldn't be alone.

"Lia!" Carson yelled before I could get too emotional. With those headphones on, he probably had no idea how loudly he was talking.

I excused myself as I walked past a few people to get to my seat. My cheeks warmed at the continued glances at my outfit. "Hi, Mr. and Mrs. Miller. Hey, Carson." I took my seat next to Pierce's brother.

"Oh, Lia, thank God," Mrs. Miller said. Worry was etched into the lines around her eyes. "Do you know where Pierce is? He's not here yet, and no one can get a hold of him. He texted me to say he's fine and he'll explain later, but he would never miss a game! Where is he?"

I knew about that text, because I'd been the one to type the response while Pierce drove. "He's here," I said quickly, just so that worry would melt away. "We got here together. And he's okay."

"Thank God," Mr. Miller said, looking like a thousand pounds had just been removed from his shoulders.

"If he's here, where is he? The game starts in three minutes!" Mrs. Miller bit at one of her nails, which looked super short already.

There were several NTDP players on the ice, but none of their jerseys had Pierce's number. He also wasn't on the bench. The team's head coach was also missing. Maybe he was so mad at Pierce for being late he wasn't going to let him play? He couldn't do that when the Wings's scout was going to be here, could he?

"Lia, look," Carson said, much too loud again.

He held out a Lego book for me to see. I made the appropriate "ooo" and "ahh" noises, happy for the distraction. If Pierce wasn't going to play, there was no way I could stay and watch this game. Flashbacks from the last hockey game I'd been to were already hitting hard and fast.

As the clock counted down, my pulse sped up. Where *was* he? Just as I was about to give up, to apologize to Pierce's parents for the fact that he wasn't here and I couldn't stay, Pierce walked out to the bench, wearing his skates and carrying his helmet.

"There he is!" I said.

Mr. Miller gave a relieved sigh. "Thank goodness."

Pierce skated across the ice, scanning the rows of seats until he found us. He smiled and winked at me and gave his parents what appeared to be an apologetic wave. Then he put on his helmet and skated around, taking a few quick laps to warm up before the buzzer announced the end of the warm-up period.

"Coach is starting him," Mrs. Miller said with some combination of tension and excitement as all but two rows of players left the ice. As hard as it was for Pierce to lose game after game, it must have been just as hard for his parents to watch.

The announcer introduced the two teams and their starting players, including Pierce, and the puck was dropped. My stomach was in knots. The lace on my skating dress was too tight around my neck. I could still hear the crack of the collision from my dad's last hockey play. It would take almost nothing for that to happen again to someone else. For another family's world to be turned upside down.

"Are you okay, Lia?" Carson asked.

It took a second for me to realize that he wasn't yelling anymore. When I turned to him, he had pulled the headphones tentatively off his ears and was looking at me with concern. It was only then that I realized I was breathing shakily and wringing my hands. "Yeah," I said, but then one of the NTDP players was checked into the boards right in front of us and I flinched hard. "I'm okay." The words weren't very convincing.

Carson pulled the headphones off his head, messing up his long hair. "I know it's loud." He extended the headphones to me. "Do you want to borrow these? They work good."

My heart melted. "Carson, thank you, but you need your headphones. That's okay."

He considered. "I think I'm okay. Maybe we can take turns using them."

I looked over Carson's head to Mr. and Mrs. Miller. Despite the game going on in front of us, they were both looking at me with obvious hope in their expressions. Maybe this was the first time Carson had offered to be without his headphones. They needed me to take them.

So I took the pair from Carson, adjusted them slightly, and thanked Carson before putting them on my own ears. I felt so ridiculous sitting there in my skating dress with a pair of neon green headphones on my ears, but the smile on Carson's face and the tears in Mrs. Miller's eyes were worth it.

The headphones were as effective as the soundproof practice room I'd shared with Embry. The only thing I could hear was my own heartbeat. If I closed my eyes, I'd never believe I was in a hockey rink. When I turned my attention back to the game, it only took a few seconds before another player was checked, but I didn't flinch. I didn't hear it. I looked over at Carson and he gave me a thumbs up before going back to his Lego book.

As I continued to watch play after play with no one getting hurt, the echo of my pulse in my ears got slower and slower. I was able to sit still and stop wringing my hands. Something about the silence seemed to make the sound in my memory quieter, too. What had happened to my dad was a fluke. Pierce was going to be okay. Yes, I was nervous for him, but in the quiet I was more worried about his performance than anything.

Less than a minute was gone off the clock when Pierce got the puck and headed in the direction of the opponent's goal. He evaded two defenders, lined up his shot—I could almost see him reading the goalie—and slapped the puck right into the net. He made it look easy. He made it look like the Pierce Miller everyone knew and loved. The crowd erupted in cheers, but I couldn't hear them.

When I looked over at Carson, he had tensed up, his hands halfway to cover his unprotected ears, but then the crowd returned to their seats and Carson's hands returned to his lap. It was like he realized everything was going to be okay, too.

I removed the headphones to a rush of sound. "What do you think?" I asked Carson. "Your turn?"

He looked between the headphones and his parents, as if deciding what the right move was. "Maybe I'll just hold them in case I need them," he said.

"I think that's a great idea," I said and handed them over. "Thank you for letting me borrow them."

Mrs. Miller mouthed a grateful "thank you" to me, but it was me who should have been thanking them.

By the time the first period ended, the score was four to nothing. Pierce had scored three of the four goals and made some pretty strong defensive plays. Pierce Miller was back.

When the buzzer sounded at the end of the game, solidifying an impressive win for NTDP, Pierce skated over to us. He lifted the necklace from beneath his jersey and held it up to me before tucking it safely back into place. Somehow I knew my dad would be so happy I was able to watch a game again and that part of him was there, helping Pierce play his best. Tears filled my eyes, but they were happy tears.

Everything was going to be okay.

Epilogue

"Bye, Miss Lia," Olivia said, giving me a hug. "I hope you win your competition."

I'd placed third in my senior regional competition, which meant I was off to sectionals and hopefully nationals. Several of the workshop kids, Olivia included, had made me good luck cards covered in crayon-drawn medals and figure skates. "Thank you," I said. "And I hope to see you in a competition someday!"

The little girl grinned and turned to Pierce. He crouched down so she could give him a hug. "Bye, Mr. Pierce. Thank you for helping me skate."

"Anytime, kiddo. Keep up the hard work."

Olivia's mom thanked us, and they walked out of the rink, the last people closing the door on our workshop for the last time.

"Phew," I said, leaning back against the boards. "Done."

"We made it," Pierce said, leaning next to me. I wondered

if either of us would have enough energy to make it off the ice. It turned out that the better the kids got at skating, the harder our teaching jobs got because we had to keep up with them.

"Everything's put away," Adam called from the Zamboni bay where he'd placed all of the cones and other materials we'd used. It turned out that Adam and Uncle Drew had been kind of awesome substitutes for me and Pierce. The kids loved Adam, and even more important, he seemed to like it, too. He liked being back on the ice and having responsibility, and he *especially* liked getting paid. Maybe school wasn't his thing, but maybe that was okay as long as he found *something* to keep him out of trouble. I'd already heard Mr. Kozlov mumbling something about finding my brother a summer job.

"Thanks, Adam," I called.

"I'm getting celebratory last-day nachos from the snack bar," he called back. "You guys want anything?"

"Mmm, nachos," Pierce said, patting his stomach.

"Nah, we're good. Thanks," I called back.

Pierce scoffed at me. "Hey. I want nachos."

"No, you don't. You have playoffs coming up. 'Eat like crap, play like crap.'" Thankfully, Pierce hadn't been playing like crap lately. Not at all. But he didn't need chips and fake cheese to change that.

"I'm not worried about playoffs. Scott Butler wants me to play for the Wings regardless of whether we win the championship or whether I eat nachos for lunch."

"He said those exact words, huh?" I asked.

Pierce just grinned. "Close enough."

I waved Adam off. "Go ahead. We'll meet you out there."

"Suit yourself," Adam said before skating off the ice.

After the door clicked shut, Pierce and I were alone. He slid down the boards a few inches, erasing our height difference so he could rest his head on my shoulder. I let him, and looked out over the ice. After our first workshop, the ice had looked barely touched after being under the skates of kids who spent more time on their butts than their feet. Now, it was completely torn up from twenty-something future figure skaters and hockey players. Success.

"Next time I let Mr. Kozlov talk me into something, I'm going to make sure it's not something this exhausting," Pierce said.

"Me, too."

"But if it wasn't for the workshop, I'm not sure me and you would be me and you."

"Probably not," I agreed.

He kissed my neck in that spot right beneath my ear and stood to his full height again. "Do you know what I'm *not* too exhausted for?"

I suspected. I hoped. But I put on my best innocent voice and asked, "No, what?"

He turned to face me, placing one hand on each side of the boards next to my hips. Then he leaned in and kissed me. His lips were warm despite the cold air. But when his hands slipped up under my shirt, his fingers were freezing, and I gasped against his mouth.

"Too cold?" he murmured.

I adjusted his hands so they were low on my hips, but on the *outside* of my clothes. "There," I said. "Much better."

"Do you know what's funny?"

"What?"

"I know you picked the username Superfan to be ironic, but it turns out *I'm* the super fan of *you*."

I reached up, wrapping both hands behind his neck. "You're ridiculous."

He smiled that dimple-filled smile and kissed me again.

Pierce Miller kissed me.

I hoped I'd never get used to that.

Acknowledgments

To Heather Howland–thank you for loving this story and for the time and effort you put in to make it shine.

To Mom and Dad–thank you for always supporting me, whether it's on the ice or in between the pages of a book.

To Kristi Kay–thank you for coffee dates and road trips and being someone I absolutely couldn't do this "writing" thing without.

To Julie C. Dao–thank you for all of the encouragement and well-timed emails with kind words that mean more than you know.

To Kat Ellis–thank you for being so incredibly supportive since I started this journey and at every step along the way.

To Sue Winegardner–thank you for sharing your wisdom and always being willing to listen and help.

To Ann Hayes–thank you for teaching me all about commas (and plenty of other things, but mostly commas).

To you, reading this book–thank you for your time and support.

About the Author

Erin is a young adult author from North Carolina. She is a morning person who does most of her writing before sunrise, while drinking excessive quantities of coffee. She believes flip-flops qualify as year-round footwear, and would spend every day at the beach if she could. She has a bachelor's degree in mathematics, which is almost never useful when writing books.

Discover more of Entangled Teen Crush's books...

THE BOYFRIEND BET
a *Boyfriend Chronicles* novel by Chris Cannon

Zoe Cain knows that Grant Evertide, her brother's number-one nemesis, is way out of her league. So naturally, she kisses him. She's thrilled when they start dating, non-exclusively, but Zoe's brother claims Grant is trying to make her his "Ringer," an oh-so-charming tradition where a popular guy dates a non-popular girl until he hooks up with her, then dumps her. Zoe threatens to neuter Grant with hedge clippers if he's lying, but Grant swears he isn't trying to trick her. Still, that doesn't mean Grant is the commitment type—even if winning a bet is on the line.

THE GIRLFRIEND REQUEST
a novel by Jodie Andrefski

Emma is tired of being cast in the role of the girl next door by her best friend Eli. So Emma creates a fake Facebook profile in the hopes of starting an online friendship with Eli, which would hopefully lead to more. From friend request to In a Relationship--it all seemed so completely logical when she'd planned it. Two best friends, one outlandish ruse. Their status is about to become way more than It's Complicated...

Winging It
a *Corrigan Falls Raiders* novel by Cate Cameron

Natalie West and Toby Cooper were best friends growing up, on and off the ice. But when Toby's hockey career took off, their friendship was left behind. Now Natalie has a crazy plan to land her crush—and she needs Toby's help to pull it off. When Nat asks Toby to be her fake boyfriend, he can't say no. But Natalie's all grown up now, and spending time with her stirs up a lot of feelings, old and new. Suddenly pretending to be interested in her isn't hard at all…if only she wanted him and not his enemy.

The Truth About Jack
a novel by Jody Gehrman

Dakota McCloud pours out her heart on a piece of paper, places it in a bottle, and hurls it into the ocean. Loner and piano prodigy Jack Sauvage finds the bottle washed up on the beach and responds to Dakota's letter—only he can't admit who he really is. Or even that they live in practically the same town. With each letter, they're slowly falling for each other. Now Jack is trying to find a way to make this delicate, on-paper romance happen in real life…without revealing his deception.

Also by Erin Fletcher...

PIECES OF YOU AND ME

WHERE YOU'LL FIND ME

CPSIA information can be obtained
at www.ICGtesting.com
Printed in the USA
FSHW02n1955200918
52442FS

9 781682 813164